New Fiction

By The Fire's Light

Edited by

Rebecca Mee

First published in Great Britain in 2001 by
NEW FICTION
Remus House,
Coltsfoot Drive,
Peterborough, PE2 9JX
Telephone (01733) 898101
Fax (01733) 313524

SB ISBN 1 85929 036 1

FOREWORD

When 'New Fiction' ceased publishing there was much wailing and gnashing of teeth, the showcase for the short story had offered an opportunity for practitioners of the craft to demonstrate their talent.

Phoenix-like from the ashes. 'New Fiction' has risen with the sole purpose of bringing forth new and exciting short stories from new and exciting writers.

The art of the short story writer has been practised from ancient days, with many gifted writers producing small, but hauntingly memorable stories that linger in the imagination.

I believe this selection of stories will leave echoes in your mind for many days. Read on and enjoy the pleasure of that most perfect form of literature, the short story.

Parvus Est Bellus.

CONTENTS

Rustler

Alwyn James

Sleepy old Nant-y-mynydd was just coming to life as I opened up the police station ready for another day's work. I hadn't even sat down when the phone started ringing.

'They've been at it again,' cried an irate voice. A voice I recognised as that of Tom Davies, a farmer from off the hill.

'How many this time?' I asked, knowing that he'd lost some fifty ewes over the last month.

'Must be at least twenty. They've even taken my best ram this time.' He was obviously upset and I didn't blame him. Those sheep were worth a lot of money. 'I found some tyre marks in the mud,' he continued. 'Don't know if they're any good to you. '

Within twenty minutes Constable Peter Ringer and I were at the scene. Tom Davies was there and boy was he in a foul mood. Sure enough there were tyre marks, so we covered them and arranged for our Scenes of Crime Officer to attend and to take plaster casts of them.

'They were taken sometime during the night,' bawled Tom. 'What are you lot doing? You should be out looking for these people not sitting in your warm police station.'

I tried my best to calm him down, but to no avail. 'We'll do our best,' I assured him but he wasn't listening.

After we'd had a description of the animals, the markings and ear tags. we returned to the police station. Details of the theft was circulated to all police stations in the area and all the local auctioneers were given details.

Over the next few weeks we visited every sheep market for miles around. But whoever was responsible for taking the animals was making sure that they were being kept out of sight.

Nant-y-mynydd is a farming community on the English/Welsh border where news seemed to travel fast. This suited my purpose, as I wanted to spread the word that we were going to flood the area with police and that we were determined to stop the theft of sheep. I also wanted them to know that it wouldn't be safe to move after dark because the police would be stopping and checking all vehicles. My ploy seemed to work, because the sheep rustling stopped. We had the cast of the tyre marks, but they were no good without a suspect.

I worked long and hard on that case, attending markets and mixing with members of the farming fraternity. Some of the farmers were most helpful and would have given me the name of the thief if they'd known who it was. But the general agreement was that they didn't have a clue. Generally speaking the majority of farmers are extremely honest and it goes against the grain when one of their members start stealing.

It was about this time that I got a telephone call from a colleague of mine on the regional crime squad. He told me that they had a big job on and he thought I could help. He wouldn't discuss the matter over the telephone, but we made arrangements to meet. Having worked for some years on the squad, I was familiar with the workings and with most of its members.

The White Lion was nearly empty as I shook hands with D/S Des White and WDC Christ Townsend. Over a pint of beer, they explained that a good informer of theirs, had introduced them to a villain who stole lorries from motorway service stations.

'He doesn't know what's inside them until he delivers them,' they explained. 'We've met him and agreed to buy the contents. Don't know what it'll be. We didn't tell him where to deliver the lorry. But we said we'd get back to him. That's where we hope you can help. We're looking for an empty farm or a disused works or somewhere like that. It's got to be enclosed so that once he's in, he'll have a job getting out.'

'Yes, I know a place like that,' I said. 'But I'd have to get the go ahead off the owner.'

'No problem,' said Des White. 'But make it soon. We've got to get back to that fella.'

By lunchtime the following day I'd got permission off the owner of a disused plastic factory. He was most helpful and didn't even want to know my reason for asking. I did tell him that I would give him the details later. Des White was delighted and promised that I would be involved in the arrest.

'I'll let you know what's happening,' he said. 'Chances are we won't know anything until the fella's nicked the lorry. He'll probably give us a ring when he's on his way.'

The following day we all met at the disused factory.

'This is ideal,' said Des. 'A short drive into the place and no escape route and there's plenty of places for the boys to hide. This is just what we were looking for.'

The next hour was spent planning and discussing our actions if and when the lorry was driven into the factory yard. We then adjourned to the local pub and sampled some real ale.

'Like old times,' I said, sipping the amber liquid.

'Yes, it is,' said Des. 'You missing life on the squad?'

'Not really,' I replied. 'There's enough crime around here to keep me busy and most importantly I get to sleep at night. No more clubbing and pubbing for me.'

It was over a week later when the call came from Des White. 'It's on,' he said. 'The fella's nicked the lorry. He's just left Birmingham and he's heading our way. Should be at the yard in about two hours. I'll pick you up in about half an hour.'

The trap was set. There were detectives hidden in buildings and others in parked cars on the main road. I was standing in an old toilet where I had a good view of the entrance and yard. Des and Chris Townsend were sitting in their car ready to meet the driver of the lorry.

The tension was electric as the call came that the lorry was turning off the main road. It was at this point that I remembered why I had enjoyed my time on the crime squad. Very few police officers get involved in police work like this. This was exciting stuff and it sure got the adrenalin pumping.

The enormous pantechnicon stopped with a squeal of brakes. The driver, a short scruffy individual got out and walked to meet Des White.

Before he could get within ten yards of Des, he was surrounded by four heavily-built detectives. He struggled violently to no avail and the expletives coming out of his mouth were unrepeatable. He was continually threatening to kill Des and Chris even though he was now handcuffed and sitting in a squad car.

'Let's have a look at what we've bought,' said Des, a broad grin on his handsome features. The lads soon had the rear doors open and were inside checking the load.

'It's full of computers,' exploded one. 'This load's worth bloody millions.' He was right of course. It was worth an enormous amount of money. This was a good pick-up.

The arrested man was whisked off to the squad office to be interviewed and processed ready for his appearance at court the next morning. There wasn't much hope of him getting bail. The value of the load alone would make this a serious case. As it turned out, he also admitted taking another nine loaded lorries. So he wouldn't be seeing the light of day for some time.

Christmas had come and gone and by now we were well into May. It was about then that I received a visit from Tom Davies, the farmer from off the hill.

'Can I speak to you in confidence Sergeant?' he said, as I invited him into the police station.

'That's a silly question,' I said. 'You know you can trust me.'

'It's them sheep of mine,' he continued. 'I reckon I got a good idea who took them.'

'What makes you think you know?'

'I got no proof, but there's lambs on a field not far from here and I'd swear that the father is my ram that got stolen.'

Knowing a little about farming, I realised that nearly all farmers can identify each sheep by their looks. This may sound strange to most people, but it is absolutely true. I continued, 'What makes you so sure your ram was the father?'

'I can tell. The lambs are the spitting image of him and they've all got that tinge of black on the tail.'

'This sounds good, Tom, but I doubt if a court would convict this fellow on that evidence.'

'I knew you'd be like this,' he cried. 'Whose bloody side are you on?' Tom Davies was a decent sort of man, but there was no doubt he possessed a fiery temper. It took some time, but I eventually managed to persuade him that to take a thief before a court, you had to have concrete evidence and concrete evidence we didn't have at this time.

'I'm giving you the thief Sergeant,' he continued. 'It's that bloody Dennis Jones from Lower Sarn farm. I've suspected him for a long time. But now I'm sure it's him.'

'What about the ram?' I asked.

'No sign of him. I've even looked around the buildings on Tuesday, when Jones was at market. He's got rid of it somehow.'

'We'll do our best,' I assured him.

'If you find him,' exclaimed Tom, 'you'll know it's him. He's got a scar on his scrotum. Did it when he was a yearling.'

'That's excellent, Tom. If only we knew where to find him. Could be that Jones has sent him somewhere to winter.'

Over the next few days I spoke to many of my local parishioners. They all seemed to know of Dennis Jones and the general opinion was that he was a rum character. Not a man to trust.

Later that day I paid a visit to the local auctioneer. A man I knew quite well.

'Yes, we arrange land for the farmers to winter their sheep on,' he said. 'why do you ask?'

'You fix anything for Dennis Jones?'

'Yes, I think we did. Hang on, I'll check for you.'

Sure enough he had arranged for Jones to send his sheep to a farm some fifty miles away. I thanked the auctioneer for his help and decided to take the bull by the horns. I contacted Tom Davies and together we visited the farm where Dennis Jones was wintering his sheep.

I introduced myself to the farmer and together we inspected the sheep on his farm.

'There he is,' exclaimed Tom, literally bouncing with excitement. It took some doing, but eventually we caught the ram and sure enough the scar described by Tom was clearly visible. The farmer told us that he didn't know who owned the ram, as many owners sent him sheep for the winter. My heart dropped as I realised that we were still unable to connect this ram to Dennis Jones.

'There's only one way,' said I. 'We'll take the ram with us.' The farmer wasn't very happy, but he didn't have much choice.

Early next morning I got in touch with the Nant-y-myndd vet. Together we obtained a blood sample off the ram and then we visited Lower Sarn farm where after a load of abuse we obtained a number of samples off the young lambs. Dennis Jones was fuming and was continually threatening and verbally abusing myself and the vet. He can say what he likes, I thought to myself. If the DNA tests prove positive he's going to be eating porridge for a long time.

The samples were sent off to the Forensic Science Laboratory and after a week we received the good news. The lambs owned by Dennis Jones had been sired by the stolen ram. We'd got him fair and square.

Dennis Jones was arrested and charged but continually pleaded his innocence. News soon sped to all four corners of Nant-y-myndd.

I couldn't walk along the street without someone or other congratulating me on our success. Tom and I went back to the farm where we'd found the ram and we recovered another thirty-five ewes that Tom identified as his. Dennis Jones appeared at Crown Court where he pleaded not guilty to all charges. He was an obstinate individual and was purely making more work for everybody. However, we produced evidence of the tyre casts and of the DNA tests and as a result he was incarcerated for a period of four years.

I wouldn't like to be in his shoes when he's released. Farmers don't welcome a convicted sheep rustler.

EMILY

Sue Wensley

I can't believe it. Not again. I half-open my eyes and listen intently, but there is no mistake. Rain. Not the gentle rain coaxing new growth, and painting the landscape an emerald green. No. This is hard, cold, stinging rain - the kind that eats into your clothes, lashes against your face and forces you indoors.

I try to ignore the depressing sound and resolutely disentangle myself from the warm bed clothes. Mechanically, I set the morning routine in motion, and having washed, dressed, and breakfasted, I brave the elements, and drive myself to work.

'Hello, Miss.'
'What are we doing today, Miss?'

The rain becomes insignificant as twenty-four young faces crowd around me, eyes alive and shining; pencils poised, and minds open like a blind pie waiting to be filled. Just one seven-year-old girl sits quietly alone, her dark eyes watching intently. Emily observes, but does not speak.

'I had a lift in Jamie's big car, this morning, Miss.'
'Look, my tooth is wobbly.'
'It's my birthday tomorrow, Miss.'

We settle down. Twenty-five minds struggle over the patterns of the printed word, each one a goal, a pointer to success; an entry into a world of imagination where stories emerge from the page like a new-born child from labour.

We play games with numbers. Twenty-three take away six. Thirty-one add three. How many five-penny sweets can I buy for £1.00? I watch the hands strike the air, eager to provide answers to my questions. My thoughts wander. How many hands eagerly stretch out to solve the problems daily posed by the postman - the additions and subtractions of the gas bill, the electric bill and the mortgage repayment?

The rain beats against the windowpanes, accompanied now by thunder and lightning.

'Ooh Miss, did you see that flash?'
'It's scary, Miss.'
'It's the clouds fighting, isn't it, Miss?'

Emily edges closer towards me, silently pulling her long black hair around her pale face, cringing at each rumble of thunder.

It's too wet to go out to play, but the children don't seem to mind.

'Can we play Lego, Miss?'

Small fingers reach for the box and set about their intricate tasks of engineering.

'Look, Miss. I've made a train.'

A bit short on the wheels perhaps, and slightly unstable, but undoubtedly the fastest, the most modern, and simply the best train that ever existed.

I voice my approval, and am quickly drawn towards another table. A blue, red and white plastic, designer spaceship demands my attention. We all admire its shape; its size; its power; and we are surprised when the sound of a bell summons our return to work.

We cut an apple in half and study the magical pattern inside. Five tiny brown pips set within a star, each half a reflection of the other. We carefully examine the germs of future growth.

'Can we eat the apple, Miss?' inquires Sean, his hand clasping his ample body.

Amazingly, one apple is cut into twenty-five tiny pieces, each sweet mouthful tasted and savoured as if for the very first time.

'It's like the story of the five loaves and two fishes isn't it, Miss?' laughs Sarah.

We think about farmers and their continuous battle against the weather and nature, as they work to produce our food. We talk about their faithful ally, the scarecrow, who for centuries has nobly defended precious crops. We imagine big scarecrows; small scarecrows;

scarecrows stuffed with straw; scarecrows stuffed with newspapers; scarecrows who come alive and who long for brains.

'Can we draw our own scarecrow now, Miss?' demands Dylan, chewing his stubby pencil.

The room fills with paper scarecrows. All shapes and sizes. Red jackets; blue jackets; yellow jackets. Brown trousers decorated with irregular patches. Scarecrows sporting hats jauntily perched on stuffed heads at every angle. Their faces shine out from the paper; eyes looking fixedly at their creators; mouths painted in winning smiles.

'Look, mine's laughing, Miss,' says Melanie, widening her own mouth in a similar pose.
'Miss, mine's got big feet. He'll kick the birds away.'

I turn towards Emily and watch her quietly colouring. Her scarecrow looks small and shrivelled. His face is thoughtful, almost sad. I try to encourage her efforts, but Emily keeps her head bent and shoulders hunched, and continues to wield her felt pens and adorn her scarecrow with black trousers.

We collect the pictures and set them out on the table against the wall. Each one smiles benevolently at the children as they push their pencils and sharpeners into their school bags. Each one except for Emily's. Hers remains firmly in her hand. I make no comment.

''Bye, Miss. We're going to make a real scarecrow at home. He'll be alive.' Gwyn and Rob bend their heads together as they leave the room, laying plans for their masterpiece.

I am aware of Emily watching them and listening, still clutching her picture firmly.

'Goodbye, Emily,' I venture.

She raises her head and smiles - the first smile I had ever known.

'The rain's stopped at last,' I add. 'You should get home dry.'

She nods silently and walks away. I long to make further contact, but I know I cannot force her.

The next day dawns bright and beautiful. The air is fresh and the colours of the trees and hills are strong and clear. Reflections in the few remaining puddles sparkle in the sunlight. Life feels good, and I walk into the classroom with an easy step.

The children are crowding around one table.

'What's he made of?' asks Sean.
'I like his jacket.'
'Did you make him on your own?'
'He's brilliant.'

The questions and comments pour forth in a torrent. I am intrigued. What is the object of their attention?

As the children become aware of my presence, they slowly move towards their own chairs.

'Look what Emily's done, Miss,' Daniel cries.

My heart sinks. Surely Emily isn't in trouble? I turn towards her and notice a small scarecrow beautifully stuffed and dressed. sitting proudly beside her.

'He's lovely,' I say, carefully moving towards Emily's table. 'Has he got a name?'

'Pip,' she answers, simply.

'You've made him beautifully,' I add, desperately trying to build on my first point of real contact with the child.

Sarah idly clicks a castanet in the corner of the room as we study the new arrival. The rhythm is catching and my fingers instinctively join in, lightly tapping the table.

'It's like the wind catching the scarecrow's clothes, Miss,' suggests Gwyn.

Without further prompting, Emily places Pip on the table and gently flaps his loose jacket to the beating pulse.

'The movement of his jacket will scare away the birds, won't it, Miss?' says Rob.

‘Yes, I agree, smiling at Emily.

She smiles back, her dark eyes shining in a way I had never seen before.

I look at the scarecrow gratefully. Like the farmers, I feel that at last I have an ally - someone to help me scare away Emily’s insecurities and fears. The sun shines through the window. I sense it will be a good day.

A Difficult Case

Alfa

There are enough red herrings here for a fish supper

Inspector Macdonald thought ruefully, case number 25. The toughest one this month. They had uncovered very little and what there was, still didn't explain why that hauntingly beautiful corpse had turned up in a glass coffin on the stage during that last performance.

It had been hectic backstage, as always, but thoroughly enjoyable. The children were a little tired, perhaps. Two long performances on the last day, afternoon and evening, but it had been a success until then, mainly due to the outstanding singing skills of the beautiful corpse. Local radio had praised this amateur production especially, mentioned it twice in fact, during their morning programme.

The theatre was packed. Everybody expecting a night of fun and games. they ran out of ice-cream during the interval but had plenty of lemonade, coke, sweets and popcorn. Everyone was happy, looking forward to the final act. Some of the younger children in the audience were a little overwhelmed perhaps, red-cheeked, jumping up and down, noisy. The usual long queue for the toilets.

Back in their seats, familiar sweet paper rustlings, coughing here and there and then the final hush before the heavy curtain went up again.

And there she was in her glass coffin. Hauntingly beautiful. Her head on a satin cushion, eyes closed, wearing a long golden dress. In her hands a silver mirror. A present from her latest lover, so they said. She was supposed to be dead, waiting to be kissed back to life by her Prince. He did kiss her a few times. Nothing happened. The audience thought, this was the biggest joke yet and started to whistle, some shouting:

'Come on, wake up! We haven't got all night.'

Panic back stage. Something had to be done, quickly. Someone decided to bring on the children again.

'Hi-ho, hi-ho . . .'

Repeating an earlier scene. Dancing, singing, this time led by the Prince, a tall man in his late forties perhaps, still handsome, looking rather anxious but doing his best to divert attention away from the glass coffin.

'No wonder, she won't wake up for you, Grandad.'

Someone shouted from the back. Audiences can be very cruel. They want blood for their money. Mind you, they'd got it this time. Of course, at that time nobody had realised fully the horror of it all. No satisfactory explanation was given to the audience why the panto had to end so abruptly. Only, that their money would be refunded in full, the following week.

Inspector Macdonald and his sidekick had already questioned the adults of the cast, especially about the missing silver mirror. Their next task was to question the seven children, preferably in their own homes with their parents present.

A visit to the Prince's home was to be first. Emily, a rather plain little girl, the family's only daughter, opened the front door. They were led into a large, dark living room.

Rather medieval, the Inspector thought.

The Prince greeted them. He looked drawn, much older without his stage make-up.

'Do sit on that couch, it is rather comfortable. My wife is getting us some tea.'

Emily sat on her dad's knee, smiling. She liked being the centre of attention. Mum, Dad and Emily had belonged to the amateur dramatic society for a few years now.

'A serious family hobby,' the Prince explained.

It was Emily's mother who played the main part usually. But this year she became ill, just two days before the opening night. A fever and a persistent dry cough made it impossible for her to sing.

'She couldn't even come to watch the performance. Much too ill. Had to stay in bed, keep warm, poor dear!'

The Prince told the Inspector.

At this moment the door opened and a most striking, tall woman entered, carrying a tray.

Mirror, mirror on the wall, she is the fairest of them all, the inspector thought, smiling at her, thanking her for the tea.

Emily knew that all the attention would be given to her mother now, as always. She was angry, after all, the Inspector had come to speak to her. She got up and tiptoed towards the door.

'Back in a minute, Inspector,' she whispered.

When she returned she was hiding something behind her back, walked over to an enormous red armchair and sat stiffly on the edge of it.

The Inspector had watched her carefully. He had little experience with children and didn't really know how to approach Emily. But there was no need to worry any further. Emily stood up slowly, walked over to her mother, handing her a most exquisite silver mirror.

'You did tell me to bring it home, after the performance,' she smiled, then continued most innocently:

'I don't understand at all. Daddy practised kissing Snow White all afternoon. Why didn't she wake up later? She spoiled absolutely everything. You saw them practising too, didn't you mummy?'

THE RIPEST FRUIT OF ALL

Dolly Harmer

Sarah had never enjoyed housework. She should never have allowed Tony to talk her into this situation - but she had been very much in love, she remembered, and would have agreed to anything.

Now she looked at the washing-up piled high on the draining board, the washing machine filled with bed linen, and loads more work waiting to be done.

She felt like crying but there was no time. Soon the children would be home from school and there was the afternoon tea to be served and preparation made for the evening meal. And today, she must do it all herself for her 'Mrs Mop' - her mainstay, had gone to her daughter's wedding, and the girl she had come to rely on during the holidays had returned to College.

Perhaps she should be thankful to have a home from which she could make a livelihood, for after Tom had left her, without even a forwarding address, things could have been much worse. Even now that her divorce had come through, after years of waiting, she felt his loss as acutely as ever. Her early days of marriage had been so perfect and the coming of the children had only added to their joy - that is until Tony thought to give up his job in the country to try his hand as a boarding house keeper by the sea,

It was past two o'clock before Sarah got the better of the chores and allowed herself to dream of her childhood.

She had wanted to write stories, even before she could read or spell at all, even before she started school.

Her family had had no money to spare for pencils or paper, but there was a bookcase full of old books that had belonged to her grandparents. She remembered it well - polished mahogany on which no speck of dust or finger mark must be allowed to remain. It was glass-fronted, the glass kept gleaming, and she had learned to hold her breath whilst she stared inside so that she did not steam up the surface.

The books were old in years, new in condition. Grandma could barely read at all and Grandad did not have time. His job as a gamekeeper on the Estate had been more than full-time and all absorbing.

The bookcase had been a throw-out from the Manor, as had the books. Even unread they had become treasured possessions. Sarah would hold her breath and revel in the beauty of the leather bindings and gold-lettered titles. By constant looking she memorised a few of the letters she saw - all capitals of course.

'X' she knew meant a kiss, and 'S', someone had told her, was her own special letter, though it looked more like a snake to Sarah. Then there was a 'C'. That must be the new moon, surely. Once a month her mother went out-of-doors and turned over her pennies to show the new moon. Sarah understood that it should bring good fortune, but she didn't see that anything changed.

Then there was 'H' - that was the stick Dad tried to kick an egg-shaped ball over on Saturday afternoons. She liked going to watch him and having tea afterwards with all his friends was warm and exciting.

'M' was two girls holding a skipping rope for others to jump over. She had seen that when she had gone past the school at playtime.

'O' was round and reminded her of the orange she had got at the Sunday School party at Christmas, and 'Y' was like her brother's catapult.

'I love the moon,' she sang. 'XC' she wrote with her finger on the newly-planted seedbed in the back garden. She could have got into trouble for doing that, but her skill in writing had been so immature that her father blamed the cat.

'Boys and Girls come out to play,' she sang, 'and Dads too on Saturdays,' she thought, writing 'MH' with a chalk stone on the paved path. When she saw it, Mum gave her a wet scrubbing brush.

'Go and wash that muck off the path,' she said.

When Sarah wrote 'OY', she was thinking of her brother and his catapult last Christmas. She wrote it in autumn leaves that soon blew away.

The worst thing she did, from a grown-up point of view, was to write all six letters on her bedroom wall. She wrote them just before Christmas when love and games and presents were all mixed up together in her mind. She licked her finger and wrote them with her spit and Mum caught her doing it. Then, she was in bad trouble with Mum, but luckily her finger had been licked clean before she wrote and when Dad came in from work, it had dried and gone.

'I'm sorry I licked the wall,' she said.

How could a grown-up have known her efforts were the early works of a would-be authoress?

When Sarah started school she had learned her letters very quickly and before the other children were even able to copy their names, she was writing her own News. She was made to read out to the whole class what she had written and soon the private life of her family was known to all.

Best of all, she loved story time at the end of each afternoon. It was best if there was a prince and a princess, who lived happily ever after.

When she could write well enough without help, she decided to write a story about two rabbits, who mated and had babies. Because her father was a gamekeeper like her grandfather, she was accustomed to talk about bucks and does and mating - she was not aware of any taboos.

Her city-bred teacher, unused, as yet, to country ways, and a spinster, for whom rabbits conjured up a picture of Beatrix Potter creations, was shocked by her story - and in her first horror, she quite frightened Sarah. Her teacher-training should have warned her to think before she spoke.

Sarah couldn't understand her criticisms - 'not nice'. 'Obscene', 'disgusting', were words she had never heard - but Miss Bray's face left her in no doubt that, for some reason, her story was unacceptable.

That incident had changed her personality. From a happy outgoing child, she became a shy withdrawn one.

However, she was a gifted child, a pupil who couldn't help learning, so that she gradually gained control of her feelings enough, so that by the time she graduated to the third form of her Senior School, she took with her a report for good behaviour and average ability.

Because she now felt more secure, she let her flair for writing have full rein in her first English homework in the new class. When the work was returned, the teacher held Sarah's back.

'I'll see Sarah in break time,' said Mr Blacker.

He had read her work. It was so delightful, that he dismissed out-of-hand the thought that Sarah could possibly have written it herself.

'No child of thirteen could possibly have written this,' he told Sarah. 'Either you got someone older to write it for you or, more likely, it's plagiarism.'

Sarah did not know what plagiarism meant, but she knew it was her own work, and said so. Mr Blacker did not believe her. He told her to be more original next time. And 'next time' meant now! She was kept in detention.

Sarah seemed to have done wrong again, although she didn't understand how. She sat down under Mr Blacker's watchful eye and wrote a different story. In truth, this had been more akin to plagiarism. She changed the simple story her friend had written about a girl and her dog going out in the park in the summer into a story about a boy and his cat staying indoors in the winter. She used very simple words and kept it to one page only.

'That's better,' said Mr Blacker, and he wrote 'C' on it.

'You can go now,' he said, 'but never again give me work like that other lot.'

And Sarah didn't. She managed to turn out just passable work like her friend until she left school, and gradually she became more secure again. Her final report described her as 'quiet and shy' and her work as 'just adequate'.

Sarah still felt like a writer inside and now she was grown up she began to write down things she had wanted to write when she was still a child.

She had just started on a novel when she married Tony, a trainee gamekeeper, then, under her father. She stopped writing for a time as she coped with her wifely chores and the arrival of the two children in quick succession.

When both the children were at school, she had more leisure. She decided to attend a Further Education Class in the next village. On Wednesday mornings she saw there was a class called 'Creative Writing'. She looked no further and signed on.

There were fifteen students. They came from all walks of life. There was the doctor's wife, who was keen on gardening - flowers especially. She saw her characters as hardy annuals and their personalities as colours.

There were three pensioners. One had lived an exciting and dissolute youth racketing around the world; one was a local preacher who saw the hand of God in every situation; the third had a clutch of grandchildren and saw the world through their eyes.

The industrial nurse and her hospital counterpart supplied authentic medical details that were a help to the other would-be writers. The journalist helped to leaven the ponderous style adopted by some students. Two unemployed youths brought a new perspective and gave realistic social comment to ongoing life today.

The farmer's wife, too, was able to supply helpful information on the countryside, and the off-duty policeman kept us in line with the law. Three young mums and Sarah completed the class.

Sarah loved the classes and the discussions within them. She read all the recommended books, and each week wrote something herself. She found the stories she had written before her marriage and rewrote them in the light of her new experiences - but she never took a contribution of her own to the class.

There came a day when the tutor insisted every student must submit a piece of work before signing on for the next session. Sarah went through her writings. First she considered her Harvest poem

'Gently she laid herself upon the earth
Awaiting her mate.
He did not come.
Without his help she could only bring destruction.
The longer she lingered, the worse things grew
Leaving rot and decay in her wake.

When he came to see his beloved
He saw that she had preceded him.
He restored the devastation.
But as he stayed, burning with passion
He left his own trail of desolation.

At last they came together
Bathing the Earth in their beauty
Rejoicing in the true marriage
Of Rain and Sun.'

That would be topical, but poetry was not really her scene.

There was the story of the boy who'd run away and taken his tent. So well-versed was he in Cub lore that it took an ordinance survey map and careful tracking by his parents to catch up with him.

But when she thought of reading out loud she was filled with dismay and uncertainty. Tony noticed and tried to bolster up her confidence.

'You can do it,' he said. 'And how about writing about us? You know how we look and how we were brought up. Imagine we lived elsewhere - the seaside - and had different jobs - perhaps keeping a boarding house. There's a story there.'

The banging of the door woke her. She was blinded by the afternoon sunlight, streaming in the window.

'Where is everyone?' a voice called. 'How did your day go? Where are the children - not back yet?'

Sarah sat up trying to think straight.

'Oh, there you are,' said the voice, nearby now. 'Why, you've been crying. What is it, love?'

‘Tony?’ said Sarah, smiling a little, and then, still half-asleep, remembering. She wept.

‘It’s all right, love,’ whispered Tony.

‘I’m here early - remember, it’s our anniversary!’

She could not control her tears. He looked at her, considering.

‘You know you really do need a holiday,’ he said. ‘Shall we leave the kids with your mum and go off by ourselves to the seaside? We could stay in a boarding house for a couple of days.’

She was distressed.

‘No, oh no,’ she said, ‘that’s where I’ve been - working!’

He ruffled her hair.

‘What are you saying, woman? It’s not working you’ve been. Wake up!’

Now at last Sarah became really awake. She stretched up and gently caressed him.

‘Want to talk about it?’ he said.

‘Please,’ she said and told him of her dream.

The nightmare of divorce and hardship gave place to her content and she felt she could happily shelve her novel now.

She had lately had a growing feeling of fulfilment, of joy. Tony had sensed it too and hurried home from work whistling, or dropped in for an extra cuppa when his work had brought him near to home.

Only today she knew the reason and planned to tell Tony later. She told him now.

Before the daffodils danced again, Louise, or maybe Louis, would be sleeping in the cot Tony had made for their firstborn.

The Gift
Betty Hynds

As Edna Mullary closed the churchyard gate and stepped onto the path she paused for a moment to knot her woollen scarf against the swirling snowflakes. Out of habit she peered into the distance picking out with some difficulty her solid lamp-lit house at the end of the lane. She sighed thinking that at least the light looked welcoming.

The task of arranging the flowers in church had fallen to her once more this Christmas Eve. Not that she minded, most people had families to cater for at this time of the year, last-minute presents to buy, visitors to prepare for and children to amuse. She unfortunately had none of these things.

It's beginning to drift already, she mused, surveying the fallen snow as it gusted beneath holly and glistening laurel bushes flanking either side of the lane.

She recalled some of her happiest memories, when she had pulled her sister Cassie on her toboggan to collect the plump turkey for Christmas Day.

Cassie had been born late in her mother's life, when Edna was eighteen years old. Sadly her mother only lived another year, it then fell to Edna to raise her sister.

Their father, in an attempt to forget his loss, had travelled to distant places but succumbed to illness, dying whilst on board a ship two years later.

When the family solicitor read the contents of the will, the girls were both well taken care of financially, but now the only family they had were each other. Naturally Edna felt the loss of her parents the most but having Cassie filled the void.

Cassie blossomed in the loving care she received from the older sister she adored, and as she had never really known her parents her life was very happy and secure.

Enough of this thought Edna mentally shaking herself. It hurt far too much to recall the past. She could not afford to remember Cassie especially tonight.

Edna trudged the last few steps suddenly recalling it was her birthday. Sixty years old today, she thought, who would have believed it? She smiled wistfully Mother had always laughingly called her, her surprise Christmas present. Well, I will have to toast myself tonight as Annie her housekeeper had gone home for the holidays. She knew though that Annie would have left her something on the stove and a good fire to come home to.

As her hand reached toward the iron gate, Edna turned suddenly, fancying that she was not alone. You are getting senile, silly woman, she muttered, surveying the empty lane that lay white and silent before her. She pushed the gate and walked up the garden path vigorously stamping her boots before entering the porch.

Once inside the house, she busied herself. Slippers first, then soup on a tray in her favourite armchair by the fire.

Later Edna stared drowsily into the flames, too sleepy to push away memories that crowded her mind.

Her deep regret concerning her beloved Cassie suddenly flooded through her once more. She sighed, why couldn't she let it go? She knew it was too late to change anything now, it was all so long ago, twenty-two years to be precise. But every year at this time it came back to haunt her.

Edna knew deep down she had been too strict and controlling with Cassie. It occurred because she had loved Cassie so much she needed to be in every part of her life. All aspects of her personal life, pushed to one side. She was so involved with Cassie's wants and needs that she lost the one person that meant something to her. She realised that she could have had a life of her own and kept Cassie also. If only she hadn't shut Alan out, paid more attention to him. But he had given up and married someone who had obviously listened and cared about his feelings more.

Cassie had turned out just the way she had hoped. She had been kind, generous and loving with the kind of humour that drew people to her. Edna had made sure that she moved in the right circles, attended all the social functions and met the most suitable men she could manoeuvre. Cassie took it all in her stride and appeared to enjoy everything that had come her way. Edna smiled to herself as she imagined her bright-eyed sister sitting beside her, with the firelight reflecting off her fair curls, recalling what a wonderful evening she had had and relaying all the comical gossip. That was all Edna had wanted, just to see her happy and content. But she realised now that she had been very wrong, making herself expect so little from life. Because as she now knew to her cost, if that was all you expected, that usually was all you got.

It had all gone well up until the time when Cassie was twenty. Then she met someone who Edna felt was not suitable at all. A local lad about the same age named Eddie Lang. He worked at one of the village shops and began to walk Cassie home, carrying her parcels.

Edna had noticed them one day as she watched for Cassie's return from the village. She thought that Cassie had been rather a long time and stood at the front window to await her return. It was the way the young man had hold of her arm and also how Cassie looked as she laughed up into his face that set alarm bells ringing in Edna's mind.

They lingered at the gate and then Eddie watched as Cassie walked to the door. He smiled and waved before ambling off, whistling cheerfully.

Edna waited while Cassie relieved herself of her outer garments. She entered the room with a soft smile on her face, which faltered slightly as she saw Edna standing at the window. Edna asked quite sternly who the boy was. Cassie looking defensive, told her his name and where he worked. Edna warned her that he was not the sort that she should be mixing with. Cassie had gone very still for a moment, quietly answering that they were just friends. Edna restated that this was not a good idea as it might give the wrong impression to people. Cassie, much to Edna's surprise had retorted that this was her life and it should not matter what other people thought. Taken aback, Edna had then forbidden the girl to see him again. Regretfully the argument had escalated into a battle of wills, which Edna felt she had definitely lost. From then on the atmosphere in the house was never quite the same. Although Cassie was never rude to Edna again she felt that the distance between them could not be breached.

Edna tried to interest Cassie in the coming Christmas celebrations but was met by polite indifference. She felt that perhaps if there had been a third party to intervene then things might have been resolved. But as it was, neither one of them was going to give in. They had stilted conversations but a little of Cassie's warmth was missing.

Christmas Eve was usually their best time in the house. They would decorate the tree together and then celebrate Edna's birthday with a special cake made by Annie.

Edna arrived back from church as usual about six o'clock, she called out but there was no answer. She had hurried to the kitchen to check with Annie about the evening meal and to ask after Cassie. Annie told her that Cassie had left the house just after Edna that afternoon, she looked uncomfortable as she informed Edna, Cassie carried a large bag with her. A sharp pain struck at Edna's heart.

Cassie was gone of course. Edna knew deep down who she had gone with and why, although she would not let herself believe it. Her first thought being how could she get her back. She had run all the way to the village shop. She hammered at the door until someone answered. The shopkeeper told her, the young man had gone to London for good, late that afternoon. After that Edna knew she could do nothing but hope and pray that Cassie would realise her mistake and hopefully return home in the New Year.

The following week, just as Edna was trying to think of a way to find Cassie, she received a short letter from her.

Cassie explained that she was sorry she had to leave but she had to learn to live her own life. She thanked Edna, stating how much she loved her but not to concern herself. Edna had never heard from Cassie again.

A coal fell onto the hearth startling Edna into waking. She bent to her knees and shovelled the hot coal back into the fire. The carpet slid back revealing an envelope that Edna guessed must have fallen from the mantelpiece.

A late Christmas card I suppose, thought Edna. Puzzled she opened the envelope. The writing was heart-wrenchingly familiar. It began:

My dearest Edna

I know it has been so long but I hope you will forgive me for writing to you now.

I feel that I let you down badly and have been very selfish.

My life has not been a bed of roses but I would not have changed it. I married Eddie and we were happy, we were not financially well-off, but we did love each other very much. We both realised we would never have been content if we had stayed. It was difficult for us both, Eddie wanted me to be happy. Knowing that it would tear me apart to leave you, he offered to go away and never see me again but I refused. I loved him you see.

The decision was hard for me to make Edna and it cost me dearly to make it. I realised that you always put me before your own happiness and how much you had given up. But now I have to ask a very great favour of you.

I lost my beloved Eddie a few years ago, he was killed in action during the war in France. I have managed reasonably well but I have been in hospital for some while and I find myself unable to care for those close to me any longer.

For you see, I have children, a boy and a girl and they will need someone to love and guide them. If you could find it in your heart to forgive me, I can think of no one better to take on the task. Please see this as my final and most loving gift I can bequeath to you Edna.

They love you already as I have always talked about you, to them. When they arrive it will mean that I will be gone, so please love them as you loved me.

Your ever loving sister
Cassie

Edna clasped the letter to her, tears rolled unchecked down her cheeks, her mind in an utter turmoil. She could not imagine her beloved Cassie about to die, she must go to her. She must work things out clearly in her head. She rose on trembling legs and walked towards the window, steadying herself against the window sill.

The snow had stopped falling and the lane appeared beautifully still and quiet. The church was bathed in moonlight and the bells were pealing loudly as Edna noticed two people turning into the lane. She blinked twice to adjust her vision and was then able to see the figure of a tall girl, with fair bouncing curls holding the hand of the slim boy by her side.

Edna caught her breath, filled with joy and sadness at the same time. As she ran to the front door she knew that Cassie's gift had arrived.

THE MAGE'S ASSISTANT

Caterina Gallo

The bell tolled once. The day's spell-casting lessons would begin shortly. Around the hallowed halls of the Academy, she could hear the chatter of aspiring mages as they gathered their spellbooks and components to make their way to the shielded laboratories.

Picking up her own books, Kara sighed. She had been the Mage's Assistant for a year now, left her home, family and friends for this opportunity, and had been so excited that she could hardly wait. Now, each time the bell rang, she regretted making that decision.

Kara strolled out of the library and silently mingled with the young apprentices who had just finished their alchemy class. Bright, faces, glowing with the innocence of youth, looked to her in admiration.

'Good morning, Mistress Kara,' said Rufus, one of the new apprentices. He smiled as he stepped alongside her.

Kara forced a smile. 'Rufus,' she acknowledged. The other students held back expectantly; they all wanted to know if the rumour was true.

Kara continued walking, her eyes fixed firmly forward. She could feel the apprentices watching her every move.

'Mistress,' began Rufus in a voice preceded by a deep calming breath, 'will the Mage be taking the class today?'

Kara shifted her gaze to look at the boy. 'Why do you ask?' Kara enquired sternly. For the last nine months, Kara had been teaching the class herself as well as preparing the lesson plans and tests, much to her irritation. Did they think she was incapable?

Chagrined, Rufus answered. 'I heard that the Sorcerer would be visiting the classes today. I thought that perhaps the Mage would be making the effort . . .' His voice died away.

Kara clenched her jaw in anger. The Sorcerer! When was the Mage planning to tell her? She had already prepared today's lesson plan - it was too late to alter it now.

Ignoring Rufus' question, Kara strode ahead towards the laboratory. The class was assembled outside, nudging one another and whispering.

Muttering the briefest of incantations, Kara placed her flattened palm on the door and pushed. It opened. Kara entered the large oblong laboratory. Granite pillars held up the high ceiling and six long benches were set up, one behind the other, in the centre. The apprentices filed in and took their places. Kara closed the door with a sharp command, then marched towards the compound table near to the lectern.

Something was different. Instead of dozing in his chair, the Mage was at the front of the class. He appeared irritated, standing with his arms folded across his chest, crumpling his golden robe. Dark eyes bore into Kara as she walked forwards.

Unperturbed, Kara immediately started the class. As she placed her spellbook upon the lectern, she noticed the Mage had not moved. She hesitated.

'You may sit down as well, girl,' said the Mage, balancing a pair of lunettes on his hooked nose, 'I will be teaching today.'

Kara's eyes widened. 'You?' she said before she could stop herself.

'What did you say?' he sneered, towering over Kara and using his height to intimidate her.

Kara stepped back, almost tripping over her robe. She realised that the devious Mage had decided to perform his office solely to impress the Sorcerer!

The apprentices had been right. Kara could see the look of surprise on their young faces as they witnessed the Mage's fickleness.

The Mage snatched the spellbook from the lectern and scanned her lesson plan hastily. His mean eyes narrowed. 'You were going to teach them the sleep spells?' He looked up abruptly, 'you're not supposed to do that until they have mastered levitation.'

Kara bit her tongue. 'We studied that last month - they *are* ready to progress.'

The Mage's left eye twitched. 'All right,' he snapped, 'sit over there and keep quiet.' He turned his back on Kara and faced the class.

Humiliated, Kara remained rooted to the spot. She had held the class together all this time and had covered for the Mage's laziness and ineptness as a teacher. He didn't even appreciate or acknowledge her talent. The stone bench in the corner beckoned, and Kara forced her legs to move.

Tears stung her eyes as she tried to control her emotions. She was as good as any of the Academy mages or their assistants, and certainly a better teacher than this buffoon. She had tolerated his indolence, biding her time in the hope of a transfer to another class. Though Kara had tried to ignore the Mage's constant taunts and criticisms, he persistently made things extremely difficult for her.

She brushed away long dark hair which had fallen over her face, then looked up. The Mage was in full swing, dictating to the class using her notes. He had the apprentices' attentions, except one. Rufus' young eyes were fixed upon her, his little face full of empathy. Then he smiled. Kara felt lifted.

After a few moments, there was a knock at the door. The class gasped. The Mage stiffened. Kara slumped back against the wall.

'Enter!' called the Mage, raising his hand to unravel Kara's lockspell.

The door opened slowly and in came one of the other Mage's assistants. 'Master,' he said, bowing slightly, 'I have been told to inform you that the Sorcerer will not be attending your class today.'

'What!' roared the Mage, throwing Kara's notes to the floor, 'get out!' he yelled to the poor messenger.

Kara allowed herself a small smile. As the class began to discuss the occurrence, the Mage flew into a rage and rounded upon Kara, 'You did this!' he accused, waving a bony finger. 'He would have come if it wasn't for your stupidity!'
Kara felt herself flushing red. What was he babbling about now? She hadn't even known the Sorcerer was coming.

'Take over the class!' he ordered, 'I have far more important things to do.' With that, he stormed out of the laboratory, leaving Kara and the apprentices alone.

For a while, no one spoke. Kara forced herself to move and bend down to pick up her strewn notes. She was worth far more than this, but if she complained about the Mage he would see to it that she never worked as a tutor again.

A small hand appeared and picked up some of the papers. Kara looked up to see Rufus who had left his seat to assist her.

'Thank you,' Kara whispered hoarsely. 'Take your seat now, Rufus, I will continue with the lesson.'

It took great courage for Kara to continue, but she knew where her responsibilities lay.

***

The next few days grew worse for Kara. The Mage reinforced his public humiliation of her. Even out of the classroom he hounded her, and poisoned the minds of her fellow assistants with tales of her incompetence in magic. She bore it as only one who is inferior does, and continued to teach the classes for her Master. He never showed his appreciation, but constantly heckled from the corner of the laboratory. Kara knew, however, that the students respected her all the more for her restraint.

A week later, Kara found herself in a worse situation. Following a difficult lesson in which the Mage had stood over her as she worked, she accidentally shattered a bottle of sulphur. The problem was compounded by the fact that the students were learning combustible spells and the laboratory almost became a fireball.

'You fool!' the Mage spat. 'You have taught your last lesson in this Academy, girl! Get out! Out!'

Kara felt her head spinning. This was so unfair. After everything that had happened, now *she* was being punished! Trying to brush the sulphur from her robe, lest it ignite as she walked out of the protected laboratory, Kara noticed the apprentices rallying round, led by Rufus.

The Mage saw them as well. He turned sharply, and gestured with his hands. 'Sit down all of you before I turn you into toads.'

Some of the children blanched in fear, but Rufus was not intimidated. He stepped forward and placed a small hand upon Kara's stained robe. In an instant, the sulphur disappeared and the robe seemed cleaner than ever. Kara stared at the boy in wonder. She hadn't taught him that.

The Mage grabbed Rufus by the shoulder and shook him. 'Do you have a problem with your hearing, boy?'

Rufus stared at the Mage. Then Kara felt something different. Rufus was far more powerful than he should have been. A moment later, the Mage stepped back, a look of horror on his face.

'You!' he breathed, glancing from the boy to Kara, and then back to the boy again.

Rufus nodded, lifted his arms over his head and lowered himself into a ball. Hidden by his voluminous robe, no one could see what was happening, but Kara could feel the power growing from somewhere inside the child. Rising up to full height, Rufus transformed from a small boy into the tall, white-haired, green-eyed Sorcerer, complete with silver robes and staff.

The apprentices stared in awe as the Head of the Academy stood before them. Kara could not believe it; all this time, the Sorcerer had been posing as a student in her class!

The Mage recovered well. 'Master,' he bowed low and humbly, 'I applaud your talents, you almost had me fooled.'

The Sorcerer raised an eyebrow. 'And you had me completely fooled until I saw for myself what a shallow, superficial and slothful man you really are. You teach these children nothing, abuse your assistant, but still expect others to revere you.' He stepped closer to the Mage. 'You will leave this Academy forthwith. Your services are no longer required.'

The Mage seemed to cower at first, then he straightened up and, casting Kara a lingering look of hatred, chanted and disappeared behind a veil of smoke.

Kara could feel herself shaking. What would happen now?

'Kara.' It was the Sorcerer. He had a kindly face, all wrinkled and surrounded by a white beard and even whiter hair.

She bowed her head. 'Sorcerer.'

'You should have exposed the Mage,' he chided, 'there was no reason for you to cover for him.'

Kara feared that she would also be told to leave the Academy. 'I'm sorry,' she said, 'I know it was wrong. I did my best. I know the apprentices have suffered under my tutelage.'

'Nonsense,' the Sorcerer countered. 'You forget that I have been your student for some time now, and I have to say lessons have improved since my apprenticeship.' He was laughing now.

The other students were also looking hopeful as they clustered around Kara and the Sorcerer. 'Then I can stay?' she asked.

'And be the Mage's Assistant?' asked the Sorcerer. 'No, Kara. Not anymore.' He turned to leave the laboratory. The apprentices were shocked, but none more so than Kara herself. She felt as if she would die.

At the door, the Sorcerer turned, his eyes twinkling. 'I have seen enough, Kara, to know that you have earned to right to become a Mage. This class is yours.'

A Winter's Tale

D K Brough

The wind and sleet, relentless in its fury, swept over the bleak Staffordshire moorlands, where a lonely hill farmer tried to battle his way to the stone-built house that was his home. The storm had threatened all day, and his cattle were all safe in their stalls; now his task was to drive his small flock of sheep gathered from the hillsides, to the safety of the huge Dutch barn, with its outer layers of straw bales, and its inner sanctuary against the furies of nature.

He missed his dog, too old now to brave such weather, although she would have willingly done so, indeed she had begged to accompany him, when he set out.

Now as he drove the small but valuable flock through the storm, he remembered other years, one in particular, when Bess, the mother of his old dog at home, had helped him in just such a winter's gale as this, so many years ago, to bring home the flock, but she never recovered, and died in her sleep within a few months, to be buried by the back wall of the cattle shed, where she had always lain to enjoy the summer sun. Now she rested there, leaving her daughter to take over her charges.

The sleet was turning to snow now, falling deeply, and covering the paths through the rough grass and heather, the sheep were more restless, no longer knowing where to go, and he found himself tiring in his efforts to head them on to safety from the storm, which would surely engulf them, leaving them to die in the snowdrifts, as had so many before them. He knew he must go on, to stop would be fatal, and besides, the snow was deepening all the time. The flock was becoming tired, the snow on their backs and their short legs making it difficult for them to keep moving, so they tried to turn aside from the direction he was driving them.

He looked at his watch, it was now past midnight, and he knew he should have been near home by now, but the swirling snow was blotting out the sky, so he could not see the stars, or indeed anything except the blurred forms that trod before him, and it was obvious that he might be lost, with no landmark to guide his way, but to stop would be fatal so he urged the flock onwards in sheer desperation.

It would not be the first time the moors had claimed lives; only that year a party of ramblers had taken a chance by leaving the footpaths to explore for themselves, resulting in two suffering from exhaustion and one with a broken leg, for their stupidity . . . And he also recalled one year, when he was caught in the same mist, and only the sound of his cattle lowing at home, had guided him to safety.

He was not a deeply religious man in the eyes of others, few knew that he said his prayers each night; and he attended church 'only for weddings and for funerals' as he put it, but he knew from the teaching of his youth, and his own belief, that a power greater than anything else was now all he could rely on, and as he walked he began to hum the twenty-third psalm, which seemed to give him more confidence, also conveyed to the sheep, so they now plodded on more easily before him. At the farmhouse, his wife looked anxiously at the clock on the kitchen wall; it was past two now, and she knew something was wrong, old 'Betsy' on the rug before the fire, looked up and gave a low whine, as if reading her thoughts. There was nothing they could do, and even if others could have been contacted, it would be useless to search in such conditions, only endangering other lives in vain.

Out on the moors, the singer switched to 'Onward Christian Soldiers', his mind drifting back to the wartime route marches, when he was an infantryman, in the County Regiment, and how they sung as they marched. The trouble was he was young then, now, half a century on, it wasn't so easy. He also recalled the bad winter when, on such a night as this, he had got lost, eventually sending Bess home to get help. She had made it and guided them behind her to where he and the flock were resting, over two miles from the farm. Bess never really got over the ordeal, but she certainly saved him and the flock from almost certain death from exposure, or suffocation in the drifts.

This time he had no dog to rely on, he hadn't wished to take on a new pup, since he intended to retire, but somehow couldn't bring himself to leave the life he loved so much, and had kept putting it off 'for perhaps another year'.

Suddenly the sheep began to act strangely, bleating and looking behind them and he saw a black shape moving towards them. His hands tightened on the stout stick he carried, there were rumours of big cats, possibly panthers, on these moors. and although he scoffed at such nonsense, he felt uneasy, just the same. The black shape drew nearer, and to his relief, got close enough for him to see it was a dog, moving forward, and also from side to side of the sheep who now seemed to have gained confidence and were moving steadily forward; all he had to do now was to keep up with them.

After half an hour, he became aware of the lowing of cattle not far away and soon he saw the outline of buildings which he recognised as his own.

The dog continued to move the flock steadily on, even to his surprise, into the converted fold he had provided in the huge Dutch barn.

Tired as he was, he put the hurdle across the entrance, then turned to pat the dog, who surely deserved some supper, but no dog was in sight, and yet he could not see how it had left so quickly!

Slowly he made his way to the house, passing the grave of 'Old Bess' and as he did so, it was then that he realised the truth.

He had always argued with the locals that man and beast were equal, with the same purpose in life, and to serve each other, and that even food animals deserved respect, and a humane end . . . was it so strange then that his old friend of so many years should be able to return to help him in his hour of need?

Aloud he said 'Thank's Bess, you're a good lass' then went into the house, where both wife and dog greeted him with delight, he would never tell others of his encounter, but as he looked down at the old dog, she wagged her tail, as if to say 'Yes, I know!'

And there we will leave him, warm and safe, the sheep lying peacefully in the fold, with one old dog gone back to sleep, and the other gone to wherever such dogs abide. For this is a story that could be true, and you, the reader, will never know for sure.

Skin Deep

Robert D Shooter

Catching the living flame wasn't easy. On the other hand I hadn't had to do anything difficult.

It was hard in the sense that there was nothing to see, or touch, or feel, or smell, or hear. Well there was and there wasn't. It was only in those sense things if you already had caught it. Otherwise it was just silly.

My best friend at school, Simon, did have some proof of his initiation. In the bogs, when we were trying to see who could pee the highest, you could just see that his willy had been cut up. At school sports or swimming he would change in a closet as if ashamed of his cut.

Simon called it circumcision. I thought that it must come from 'sir' as in scissors or cutting. But Simon said that it wasn't that at all. He said it was a sign to show that he was special. So I said, in that case why did he hide it away? He said that he felt ashamed to show it in front of people who had not been circumcised, as they would not know the difference. I said I had assumed that was the point - showing it to those not in the know. There seemed little point in those knowing, seeing.

Simon shrugged his shoulders saying he wasn't sure but it was important to have it done in his religion, all the males had done for generations, since before the last millennium. He wasn't ashamed in the sense that it showed to those in the know what it meant. He was embarrassed that those who didn't would just laugh, or make dirty jokes, or think that he was wounded. He said that his was done as a baby even to that Saviour of my faith, that heretic Jesus.

I said that I thought that he should wash his mouth out for saying that about Jesus but he said that Jesus was circumcised as a Jew. I said I meant what he said about being a heretic and he laughed. He said that he didn't fully understand why but Jesus was not seen as useful in his religion, more of a mistake. A good intention that misfired. When I looked puzzled he said I had better ask his father for more details. All he knew was that Jesus was frowned upon. But not for not being cut up, I joked and for that he thumped me and we chased each other around the playing field.

'I know your religion sees him as a Saviour, as the Son of God, as the one bringing the word of God to his people,' Simon went on, 'but to us he let us down. He confused God's message.'

'Which one was that,' I asked.

'The one of loving your neighbour as yourself or that of loving God'. Simon said that his folks did not much like Christ's summary of the commandments. They respected the full law.

I said 'Is that what Paul is going on about in his letters? You know that it is faith not works or law that counts?'

He said that Paul was not accepted either. I said I liked Paul but said that Simon seemed to know a lot about Jesus and Paul and things for someone who professed to know nothing about them. He said that they were taught enough so as to argue against being infiltrated by Christ.

'Sounds like not being open to hearing, seeing, and sense, things like that,' I said, and he said that if I carried on he'd give me such a beating that I'd be silent for the rest of my life. I dared not say, just then, that that seemed to prove the point going through my mind. Closed to God.

Anyway, I digress. Simon, this Jewish friend, we were close friends when we kept off religion. This chap who knew so little about Christ and Christianity that if I was unsure about any detail I only had to ask him, came round to Gran's for tea one Sunday.

It wasn't done on purpose. Gran's church was having a harvest service and supper that afternoon and evening, and tea for us was in that. I was used to such a service. You know friendship, others serving you, eating and drinking, having some hymns and fellowship, and generally getting on nicely. Simon said that their Sabbath was like that but seemed surprised at us enjoying ourselves and worshipping in church. He said that he had been told on good authority that we never managed either of those. But evidence before him proved that wrong. It amused him that the menfolk had made the apple pies and were waiting on the women and children. He said that would never happen in their church, as men were more important. At that point my Grandma whispered to him that he would have at tough job helping them to bring equality to all as God had intended. Simon opened his mouth to answer but a thought stopped him. Much later on he said that he had talked with his sisters and mother. They did feel that they had nothing to contribute to worship in their synagogue and that being kept separate from men, even in the service, was a tradition that to them ignored Sophia, the female form of God. Simon said that the female of his people mourned still for the freedom God offered. He was going to make it his life's work to change it.

'You could simply change to coming to our church,' I suggested but that offer had him chasing me round the field with so much anger that I feared I may just get cut up if he caught me.

Later on, when he had calmed down, Simon joked that he may have considered becoming a Christian, if he had not already been circumcised. I pointed out, that from what he had told me, Jesus must have already been circumcised too before becoming a Christian so he had good precedence. Simon said, at his most aloof, that that was only a good precedence if you saw Jesus as of any use!

Simon went on giving lots of names that meant a lot to him, and some were familiar to me. The first was Abraham, but I could not remember all of the rest. The point being that there was a hell of a lot of cut-offs.

I said to Simon that there was not really anything I could tell him about Christianity that he didn't already know and dismiss. Simon said that I should not worry as he had learnt far more from me, and his visit to my folks' church, than any argument his religious teaching had given him. He said that he felt that he had caught the flavour of it, which had not been taught at all. He said that he would not have believed it if he had not tasted it for himself. I asked him what that was and he said that if I cannot explain it then why the hell expect him to! Which I had to admit was rather a good point. I was also glad, deep in my heart, unexpectedly, that he had caught something about God from my church that he could not explain because that said it all to me. He also mentioned about getting something from some woman called Grace in our church, but I don't know her and Grandma doesn't. Grandpa said that he thought that he did know her but refused to say so in case it got him into trouble. He had quite a twinkle in his eye at the time so I am going to ask him sometimes when Grandma is not about.

It seems that Simon's dad almost had apoplexy when he learnt that he'd been to a Christian service. Simon said that he was being grounded and forced never to see me again, except at school, but that his mother and sisters told his dad how daft he was being and that if his religion could not cope with a bit of contamination from another's, how good was it? What sort of example was that to the lad? So it seems that his dad apologised and lifted the ban. He also invited me to join a Sabbath meal and service. I was terrified, asking if that meant I would be castrated. They laughed saying that they would have died out as a race if they had to do that. Circumcision is, of course, what I meant and I need not have it done as a visitor. You can't guess how relieved I was. I quite enjoyed it, especially the lamb, and said so.

So you see just how hard it is to know exactly when or how you caught that sacred flame? I would have got Simon to tell you but he says you just know that it is now in your bloodstream spreading round your body and also somehow round those in communion with you, but that explanation is just silly, isn't it?

THE UNWRITTEN STORY
M Frost

It was the small island that intrigued me. Even more barren than the February landscape it lay there, just out of reach of the shore. Far enough away to keep its secrets, but close enough to fire the imagination. There were no buildings, no trees, and no sign of life at all. Even the seabirds shunned its rocks. The small boats that used these waters hurried past, their engines chugging harder to leave the island in its wake. Why? That was the question my enquiring mind asked. I had tried to bring it in to conversation with the locals but the subject was always changed.

The one man who could have helped was a crofter living on the shore but I'd been warned not to approach him. Most days his bent, bewhiskered figure could be seen pacing the water's edge. Always alone he would glower at anyone who passed close to him, his dark piercing eyes reached right into one's soul. Children were frightened into bed by 'If you're not good Tom Mackay will get you!' Even the bravest of boys kept well away. I knew, by a remark that was let slip in the pub one night, that somehow Tom's strange ways were connected to the island.

I am a perverse character, I know that. I didn't want to follow the herd and ignore him without knowing why. Surely the man, forbidding as he was, hadn't always been that way. A journalist for the last thirty years I could sense a good story and I couldn't let go. I was staying at a small guesthouse run by a widow and her aged mother. It was an excellent choice. The bed was comfortable, the food wonderful and the two ladies treated me like one of the family. Usually, after a hearty breakfast, I would take myself off for a walk. Even in the depths of winter the countryside was beautiful, and most important, in my opinion, was the fact that the tourists had not yet arrived. It was strange, but whichever direction I set off in I would, somehow, finish up on the shore staring out at the island.

It was the last day of my short break and the weather decided to let me down. A heavy mist had formed and the forecast looked anything but good. It was the kind of day to settle by a fire in a comfortable armchair. After lunch Mary, my hostess, retired to her room with a migraine and it was her mother who brought the coffee. I knew she was always ready for a chat and I thought I'd make one last try at solving the mystery that everyone in this quiet valley guarded so well.

'Sheena' I said to her, 'Why not bring another cup and share the coffee with me.' I'd bought an excellent bottle of malt whisky from the local distillery and now seemed as good a time as any to break the seal. 'We could maybe have a dram, or two, to keep out the cold.'

'You're a lad after my own heart,' she said, pulling up a chair. Her willingness to stop and chat often drew a disapproving glance off her daughter and I knew it wouldn't take much to loosen her tongue. It was, in fact, Sheena herself who brought up Tom's name.

'You've been wondering about Tom, haven't you?' she asked.

'How do you know that?'

'Ah,' she said, shaking her wise old head, 'I've seen you sitting by the lake just staring at him.' She pulled her chair closer to the fire. 'But he wasn't always that way you know. I remember a tall handsome young man with a shock of black curly hair.'

'What changed him?' I asked curiously, 'Was it something to do with the island?'

There was a long silence before she said, 'Some would say he got what he deserved.'

I poured us both another drink.

'Tom was a bad lot,' she said, 'Just like his father and his grandfather before him. Never did an honest day's work in their lives, any of them. Poaching, smuggling, thieving was second nature to them. They'd rather have a bent shilling in their pockets than a straight pound.' She gave me a wry smile, 'But in spite of all that I had a soft spot for him.'

'What happened to him, Sheena?' If I was going to find out about the island I knew this was my last chance. 'Did he go out to the island?'

She nodded her head. 'Aye, lad, he did and much good it did him.' She turned and looked directly at me. 'Many years ago the Laird from the big house put a curse on the island. His only daughter had run away with one of the workers from the estate. He searched the whole village convinced someone here had helped them.'

'And had they?' I asked.

She shrugged and carried on.' Eventually word got to him that they were hiding out on the island. You see at the far side there's a small cave. The youngsters had sailed around and tied the boat up there, that's

why they weren't seen from the shore. Anyway someone in the Laird's pay told him what had happened and the Laird went out there with two of his men. He was struggling to get his daughter into the boat to bring her back when she jumped over the side into the water and disappeared. They searched, and searched, but never found her body.'
'And the young man?' I asked.
'Rumour has it,' she continued, 'That they beat him to death and left him there. Some say that when the wind's blowing you can hear the young man's screams.'
'Surely that's just the sound of the gulls?'
She didn't answer, just shrugged and gazed down into her glass.

I bent down and built up the fire although it wasn't the lack of flames that had brought a chill to the room. Sheena's story, as eerie as it was had not cleared up the mystery of Tom's demise and I couldn't leave until I knew the full story. 'Tell me about Tom' I said.
She gave a sigh. 'We don't like to call our own, you know, and as bad as he's been, he's still one of us.'
'Sheena,' I said, 'You're the only one who's had a charitable word about him. Why is that?'
She pushed her greying hair away from her face and her expression softened. 'Folk round here forget how generous he was. They were happy enough taking his handouts if they were hard up, even though they knew it was ill gotten gains. Aye, there's plenty here took handouts from him. Now they laugh at him and mock the poor fellow.'

Sheena's chin sunk to her chest her thoughts somewhere in the distant past. Some silences can be uncomfortable and yet the elderly lady and myself, a comparative stranger, seemed content to wait for the flow to continue. And continue it did, without any prompting from myself.

'Tom had got himself mixed up with a gang from Glasgow,' she carried on. 'Real hard men they were and they were to bring him down. Two of the gang, and Tom, broke into one of the big houses on the other side of the valley. The plan was to split the loot three ways but they double-crossed him. When they got clearer and back to the cottage they turned on him. he was a big man, and strong, so instead of having a go at him they tried to threaten his wife and bairns if Tom didn't give them his share. Well, he might have been a villain but he cared for his family, and a lot better than some of them who call him. The upshot was he beat those men to within an inch of their lives.' She took a rest from her story telling and took another sip of her drink.

'What happened then?'

'They went back to Glasgow,' she replied, 'But not before they'd tipped off the police. Somehow Tom got to know the police were after him so he piled the loot in his boat and went out to the island. The plan was for his wife to fire his gun three times when the coast was clear. He was on that island for five days. When he came back he was out of his mind. Eventually his wife took herself and the bairns back to her family and he's lived like a hermit ever since.'

'Did he never tell anyone what happened on the island?' I asked. She shook her head. 'He's never spoke a word from that day to this. I don't suppose we'll ever find out, and quite honestly I don't want to know. The island can keep its secrets as far as I'm concerned.'

The next day I took one final walk by the water's edge before I set off back home. Tom was there, sitting on an upturned boat staring out at the island. The gentle Sheena was right, he had suffered enough. I would never write the story. I turned away and left the lonely man to his own private hell.

A Question Of Honour

John Notley

Not a single puff of white cloud marred the blue Mediterranean sky as Mrs Susan Carpenter, shielding her eyes from the harsh glare of the sun, stepped on deck from the air-conditioned coolness of her cabin. Even at that early hour of the morning she could feel the heat etching into her bare arms and shoulders. She stood still for a few moments, looking towards the ragged peaks of the Rif Mountains silhouetted behind the port where the cruise ship had docked at dawn. Through the thin soles of her sandals her feet sensed the fierce heat rising from the scrubbed white boards beneath them.

She moved towards the ship's rail and balanced her large brown handbag on it while she searched inside for her sunglasses. Her fingers brushed against the top of a photograph in a slim silver frame which protruded from one of the pockets. She carefully drew it out and tears welled in her eyes as she looked once again at the familiar features of her late husband. She pressed her lips to the photograph, returned it to the bag, wiped her eyes with the back of her hand and slipped the large round sunglasses on the bridge of her tiny nose.

Henry should have been with her on this cruise. They had planned it many months before his untimely death from a coronary had robbed her of his company. They had gone everywhere together, never been apart for more than a day or two throughout their married life. Henry had taken care of all the details whenever they travelled abroad; tickets, passports, travellers' cheques, everything but the packing which was Susan's department.

This cruise was to have celebrated a very special occasion - their twenty-fifth wedding anniversary. She would have cancelled it but for her doctor's insistence that she should go ahead with her plans.
'Why cancel it?' he had asked her 'What good is it going to do to dwell upon your loss? You can't bring him back. Find a friend to go with you. The holiday will do you good.'

At the time Susan had been upset by what she considered to be a callous and unfeeling remark; but now she realised that he had been right. Although the dull ache was still there, especially when she looked at the photograph, the change had done wonders for her mentally and meeting so many new people had helped her to come to terms with her grief.

She had found a companion in Mrs Barbara Sands from the bridge club back home in Scranton, Pennsylvania - a teacher of similar age and recently widowed like herself. Together they had shared the excitement, like young schoolgirls, of discovering such ports as Lisbon, Barcelona and Naples. Unfortunately the cruise was now nearing its end. *'Ulysses'* had tied up at dawn in the port of Ceuta, Spanish Morocco, the last call on the itinerary before its return to Southampton.

Barbara joined her at the rail: 'Hi Susan! sorry I kept you waiting so long, but I just couldn't find my passport.'

Together they followed the other passengers now making their way ashore to board the excursion buses which were waiting to ferry them to Tetuan. As Susan stepped off the gangway a small dusky figure pushed past her. Suddenly he snatched the handbag which hung from its shoulder strap and weaved off through the throng of tourists leaving the ship.

Susan was rooted to the spot. 'Stop him' she screamed 'My handbag, he's stolen my handbag.' It was no good. The boy had disappeared in the crowd and was nowhere to be seen.
'What shall I do?' she turned tearfully to Barbara 'I haven't any money - it was all in the bag. And my passport, everything was in there.'
'Don't worry' Barbara assured her' 'We'll report it to the Tourist Police, they'll advise us what to do, I am sure.'

They found the police office just inside the dock gates. The officer in charge was most helpful. He was a short, stout man, smartly dressed in a khaki uniform with gold epaulettes. A forbidding looking pistol hung from the shiny leather belt which struggled to encompass his generous waist. He gestured expansively with large stubby hands as he offered them seats in his cramped office on the quayside. He sat down on the opposite side of the desk, removed his peaked cap and mopped his brow with a non-too-white handkerchief. When he finally spoke to them he did so in English, uttering his words slowly and carefully with a very strong Spanish accent.

'Madame, I beg of you, please do not alarm yourself' he said after Susan had described the incident. 'I regret that this has happened many times before. However, all will be put right. Go to the City with your fellow passengers and enjoy yourself for some hours. There is much to see, I guarantee that by the time you return to the ship I will have caught the rascal responsible for this outrage and recovered your handbag. The honour of my country is at stake, The honour of my uniform also' he added.

Susan looked at him in astonishment: 'I wish I could believe that, I really do. I don't see how you can ever find him, he must be miles away by now.'

The officer arose, replaced his cap and gave a little bow:
'Please leave it to me. I have my methods. Good day ladies.'

They boarded the last bus which was taking on the few remaining passengers and left the docks. Their sightseeing tour took them first to the modern city centre around Mohammed V Square, the Royal Palace and the Archaeological Museum. During lunch they were entertained by a group of traditional folk dancers which included jugglers, firewalkers and the ubiquitous snake charmer. The afternoon was spent in exploring the narrow winding streets of the Medina. Here they bartered with the vendors over grossly overpriced handmade objects of beaten brass which would look absurdly out of place when unpacked and displayed at home.

'Oh, how Henry would have loved it here' repeated Susan many times during the afternoon. 'I am sure he would have bought one of those gorgeous carpets, he was a great one for ethnic crafts.

The two women found the colours and smells of the market fascinating as they pushed their way through crowded alleyways rubbing shoulders with sun-bronzed men from the desert leading shabby donkeys laden with goods. It seemed as if they had been transported back to Biblical times.

The sun was a ball of fire in the western sky when the bus came to a shuddering halt alongside the ship again. The police chief was standing on the quayside waiting for them. As Susan stepped down from the bus he came forward to meet her, his fat face was wreathed in a broad smile. In his chubby fingers he was swinging a brown handbag suspended by its long strap.

'I believe this is your property, Mrs Carpenter' he beamed as he handed the bag back to her. 'And I think you will find the contents all correct. I have now redeemed the pledge I gave you this morning.'
'Why. I just cannot believe it!' Susan was almost speechless. 'This is wonderful. Here . . .' she rummaged through the bag and pulled out two ten dollar bills 'you must take this.'
'No, Madame' he held up his hand in protest 'that is quite unnecessary' he said as he took the notes, crumpled them in his other hand and thrust them in his jacket pocket.
'I am only too happy to have been of service to you and I hope that you will take away pleasant memories of my country. Now you must hurry, the ship is ready to depart.'

Susan thanked him again and joined the passengers who now lined the rails as the great white liner slowly edged out of the harbour aided by two smoky, fussy tugs. She quickly checked through the contents of her bag - passport, travellers' cheques, credit cards and yes, thank God, the photograph in the silver frame. She looked at the picture with a sad smile 'I guess you were with me the whole of this trip, I couldn't bear it if I had lost you again.'

She closed the bag and waved cheerfully to the stocky uniformed figure who still stood on the fast receding quayside as the ship's siren thundered its farewell blast. The police chief returned her wave with a casual salute. Behind him a small thin brown-faced boy wearing a ragged Galabiya tugged at his jacket.

He turned around and taking a silver coin from his pocket tossed it to the lad who seized it greedily.
'Don't let me catch you doing that again Ahmed' he shouted as he aimed a cuff at the boy's head, and his left eye closed in a huge wink.

THE FLOWER MINDERS

Paddy Jupp

'Grandpa, Grandpa, here I am' called Sally, as she skipped up the garden path. She ran round the corner by the hollyhocks, then up to the tool shed and sure enough, there was Grandpa.

'Hello, tomboy' laughed Grandpa with his big crinkly smile as Sally flung her arms around his waist, 'you're late today.'

Sally giggled and squirmed as Grandpa bent down and kissed her because his moustache always tickled.

'Is my egg-in-an-egg cup ready and have you cut the bread and butter into soldiers?' asked Sally, pulling him into the house.

'Of course I have. I wouldn't forget that, would I?' replied Grandpa, puffing at his pipe and making smoke rings for Sally to catch. She loved poking her chubby finger through the middles.

Sally sat down at the tea table and clapped her hands when she saw the funny egg cosy that Grandpa had made for her. It was a silver rabbit with long ears, a funny face and a great big smile. He had two very big front teeth as well. Grandpa always made a different cosy every time Sally came to tea. They were made out of all sorts of different things and usually coloured with felt tip pens. Sally always took them home and lined them all up along her bedroom windowsill.

After tea, they both sat on the window seat watching the birds fighting over the tit-bits on the bird table.

Suddenly, Sally saw quite a big bird land on the bird table roof. He was very pretty with shiny feathers, sort of purply-blue and green and black. He was speckled all over with white spots too and in his beak he carried something very odd.

'Look, Grandpa, what sort of bird is that? Ooh, he has got something pink in his beak. Whatever is it?'

'The bird is a starling, dear, and goodness me yes, I do believe it is. It's a parcel in his beak. My word, this is a magic day' and Grandpa looked very surprised.

'Oh Grandpa, you are silly. Birds don't carry parcels' laughed Sally.

'As, that is where you're wrong, little Miss Know-all. Still, I don't know if I can tell you because he asked me to keep it a secret,' and Grandpa went and sat down in the old rocking chair by the fire.

‘I can keep a secret, really I can. I promise ever so hard’ begged Sally, screwing up her little face with the effort. ‘Tell me, tell me’ and she scrambled up on to Grandpa’s lap. Putting her hand into Grandpa’s big top pocket, she took out a brightly coloured hanky that he always kept for her to hold when he told her stories.

‘Well, a long time ago, I used to play in the fields around the little cottage where I lived. One day, I strayed further away than usual because I had seen a fox and wanted to find out where he lived. I followed him into a big wood but he had disappeared. I looked and looked but could not find him. Turning round to come home again, what do you think I saw?’

‘I don’t know’ answered Sally, ‘was it a big grasshopper?’

‘No, something much better. It was a lovely garden full of wild flowers and all around it was a circle of trees.’

‘But what about the bird and the parcel?’ asked Sally, busily twisting the hanky around her fingers so that they were all tied together.

‘I’m coming to that. My, you are impatient’ said Grandpa, untying the knot that Sally had managed to tie in the hanky.

‘Now, I had been lying on my tummy for a little while wondering how ever this beautiful garden came to be in the middle of the wood. There were lots of birds coming and going too and guess what they had in their beaks?’

‘Parcels’ squealed Sally, clapping her hands.

‘That’s right. Well, they were putting them down in one corner, then picking different ones up from another corner and flying off with them again. I thought it seemed very strange.

Just then I jumped because up popped a funny little man, right in front of my nose.’

‘What sort of funny man, Grandpa? What did he look like?’

‘He was about ten inches tall and dressed all in brown, my dear. His clothes looked as if they were made from oak leaves and on his head was a little round cap, rather like an acorn cup. In the middle of the cap was a purple berry.

‘Oh, dear, dear, this is terrible. How did you manage to get past my guards? I expect they were asleep again’ he grumbled to himself. ‘I shall have to get quite cross with them, I can see that’ and he turned as if to hurry away.

‘Please don’t go’ I pleaded, ‘not before telling me about your lovely garden anyway.
‘Well, I am very busy, you know. But still, perhaps I can spare you a moment or two only the garden is magic, you see and humans are not supposed to see it. That is why I was so surprised to see you. Still, as you *are* here and you look as if you can keep a secret, I’ll tell you. You *can* keep a secret, I suppose?’ he demanded in a very stern voice.
‘Oh, yes, yes’ I answered, very excited and bursting to know all about the garden.
‘Well,’ he began, sitting cross-legged on the tuft of grass in front of me, ‘We are the flower minders. We have to look after all the wild flowers that grow in the countryside and make sure that they grow every year for you to see. Sometimes, though, if we have a hard winter, the flowers don’t all grow again and then we find lots of bare patches about. When this happens we have to ask our cousins in other parts of the countryside to send us their spare seeds to plant in our special garden. There, the flowers grow very, very quickly so that they are ready for us to plant for the summer.’
The little man settled himself more comfortably on the tuft of grass.
‘Now, this is where the birds come in and help us. We may decide that we need ‘Monkey-flower’ or ‘Fat Hen’ seeds to fill in those bare patches and then find that we have run out of them, so we send the birds to ask our cousins if they have any to spare. If they have, the birds bring the seed parcels back to us. Often, we find inside little notes asking us for ‘Dusty Miller’ seeds, or maybe ‘Toothwort’ seeds in exchange, so you see, we help each other.’
‘Ooh, yes, just like the funny ones you show me on our walks, Grandpa’ laughed Sally. ‘Didn’t they need ‘Mouse-ear’ seeds or ‘Catsear’ ones? I like those ’specially.’
‘I’m sure they wanted those sometimes too’ smiled Grandpa. ‘Fancy you remembering those. You are a clever girl.’
‘They are nearly as good as forget-me-nots, but not quite’ said Sally. ‘Look, Grandpa, I’ve got a poor leg’ and she showed him where she had tied the hanky round her ankle.
‘Oh, dear, perhaps we had better go and see the doctor and finish this story another day’ answered Grandpa, looking very serious.

'No, no' gasped Sally, trying to untie the hanky quickly. 'It's all better now, really it is. Go on, go on' and she snuggled up to Grandpa again, waiting for him to go on with the story.

'Now then, where was I? Oh yes - As soon as the flower minders see the messages, they have to get busy, the little man told me, then asked if I had noticed the purple berry on top of his hat.

'That shows that I am the chief flower minder and everyone has to do what I tell them' he said, looking very important. The others have different coloured berries on their hats because they all have different jobs to do.'

He thought carefully for a moment, then went on -

'The black berries collect the parcels from the birds and undo them. The seeds are wrapped in flower petals, you know, that's why they are such pretty colours. Then the mauve berries plant the seeds and the yellow berries have to water them so that they start to grow quickly. We have special green water for that, you see. The white berries feed the plants with magic food so that they grow strong and straight. Orange berries gather the seeds when they fall from the flowers as they ripen and the blue berries parcel them up again for the birds to take back to our cousins; so you see, it is very hard work keeping the countryside looking as pretty as a picture.'

The little man suddenly got up again and started muttering crossly to himself.

'I must go and wake those red berries and be very stern with them. We simply cannot have any more humans learning our secret.'

Off he rushed but hadn't gone far before he turned round again and came rushing back.

'I nearly forgot. I shall forget my own head next. You must promise to keep the secret of the garden.' He looked thoughtful for a minute, then said 'As you look so kind I will let you tell one other very special person, but only one, mind you. Do you promise?'

'Oh, yes and thank you very much, but - Before I could finish, he had vanished and the garden was fading away. Quite soon there was not a sign of it at all and I began to wonder if I had been dreaming. I hadn't though because looking down on the grass where the little man had been sitting was the berry. Here it is, look, the very one' and Grandpa put a hard, wrinkled purple berry into Sally's hand.

‘Ooh, Grandpa’ breathed Sally, holding the berry carefully, ‘is it really magic?’
‘Well, I think it must be, because there was no bush or plant near me that it could have come from and the birds had all flown away.’
‘You have told me the secret too, so I must be very special’ said Sally, hugging him tightly.
‘You are my very special tomboy, so I had to tell you hadn’t I?’ laughed Grandpa, looking at his big round watch that he kept on the chain across his waistcoat.
‘Dear me, is that the time? We must get you home. Mummy will start worrying otherwise and I shall be in trouble for keeping you up late.’
‘Please, please may we go and look for the magic garden tomorrow?’ begged Sally, looking up at Grandpa with her big brown eyes opened wide.
‘Well, I don’t know. Remember, the flower minder said that it was magic, so it will be difficult to find’ said Grandpa, looking very solemn and pretending to think hard.
‘I’ll be ever so good and try to be ’specially quiet, really I will. If we look very, very hard I know we shall find it.’
Grandpa looked down at his dear little grand-daughter thinking once again what pleasure she gave him and how much he loved her. He gave her a big hug, his face breaking into his crinkly smile.
‘Oh, Grandpa, you were teasing me again, weren’t you?’ cried Sally, giving him a little smack. ‘You are always teasing me, you are.’
Grandpa laughed as Sally gave a little jump and stamped her foot, then ran out of the kitchen door.
‘Hey, you have forgotten your egg cosy’ called Grandpa as he hurried to catch her up, ‘here you are’ and he put the rabbit cosy into Sally’s right hand and took her left hand into his big brown one.

They walked down the path and round by the hollyhocks, then out of the big wooden gate and into the lane. Just around the next bend was Sally’s house, where Mummy would be waiting for them.

As she skipped along, Sally was wishing and wishing ever so hard because she just knew that if she wished hard enough, she would find the magic garden.

It's a Hard Life

Dee Twomey

It was a cold, cold night' snow was falling heavily outside. Inside the large house, Maude lay quietly in bed. She felt another pain and stifled her cry. Maude sat up and gently tapped her husband's shoulder. 'Bernard, Bernard,' she cried. 'Get Mrs Willow.'

Bernard jumped quickly out of bed and dressed, 'I'm on my way, do you want me to wake your mother up, Maude,' Maude nodded her head. Bernard knocked hard on his in-law's door. Then nearly slipped on the fallen snow as he stepped outside. There was no one in sight as he turned along into the Avenue, then left along to the Grove where Mrs Willow lived. The lights were still on' he gave a great sigh of relief as he rapped the door with his knuckles. Mr Willow, a tall stout man came to the door. 'Good evening,' said Bernard politely, 'my wife Maude is having a baby.'

'Come inside man,' Mr Willow said.

Bernard stepped inside the room, the coal fire roared. 'Mrs Willow knew someone would call tonight, she is changing,' exclaimed Mr Willow. 'Sit yourself down man.' Bernard stood on the spot, he could not move.

Mrs Willow came breezing through the door, dressed in her course blue gown with a white stiff apron over the top. 'Who have we here?' she asked in a jolly voice. Putting on her thick dark grey heavy coat.

'Bernard Dixon Mam,' he announced. 'My Maude is ready to have her baby.'

'It's a hard life Bernard Dixon,' she said.

Up the winding path, they could see all the windows were glowing with light. Bernard pushed the door open; the gaslights hissed, the coal fire crackled as they entered.

'Up here, Mrs Willow,' called out Maude's mother.

At the top of the stairs Mrs Willow turning around to Bernard,

'Your job Bernard is plenty of hot water when I call for it and towels.'

Bernard ran back down the stairs and put the largest black cast iron pan he could find on the open fire. Then went to the big cupboard to collect the towels where Maude had shown him. There was a pile of baby clothes Maude had sewn and knitted with her mother at every opportunity they found. Nappies made out of soft cotton, a row of white

towels and blankets. Bernard took an item off each pile, remembering that Maude had said they would need airing. The door opened, Maude's dad came in and sat down in his large armchair. 'It won't be long lad, with all that commotion going on,' he said.
'Sorry Pops,' Bernard said looking at him.
It's alright lad, these babies come when they want to,' said Maude's dad. 'It will be good to have another bairn around the place.'
The two men sat quietly for a while. 'Bernard,' yelled the midwife.
Bernard rushed upstairs with the pan of boiling water.
'Next time she yells Bernard, take those upstairs,' Maude's dad said pointing to the towels. 'I'm going to get dressed, the horses have to be hitched.'
Bernard paced up and down the room, not knowing what to do next. He made himself a cup of strong tea. Just as he was going to take his first sip Mrs Willow yelled 'Bernard.'
Bernard nearly dropped the cup on the floor. He picked up the towels and ran upstairs.
'Bernard,' she yelled again. He put a blanket across his arm, and picked up the pan of boiling water. He passed pops on the stairs.
'That's right lad, you've got it right, the baby clothes next.'
Bernard went downstairs, poked the fire. Pops came down the stairs.
'Any tea in the pot lad,' he asked.
'Yes Pops, although it's not very hot,' said Bernard.
'It'll do lad, it shouldn't be long now,' and patted Bernard on the back.
'I've a delivery to make at that new place where they say electricity will be made.'
Then they heard a baby cry.
'You can go up now Bernard,' his mother-in-law said.
Bernard slowly opened the bedroom door. He looked at Maude who was holding the baby in her arms. Bernard was speechless.
'Our daughter,' said Maude.
Gently, Bernard took the baby into his arms and cradled her.
'Our daughter,' he said proudly. 'She is beautiful Maude.'
'What shall we call her Bernard,' said Maude.
The baby began to whimper. Bernard gave her back to Maude. Maude unfastened the buttons down the front of her night-dress. Then put the baby to suckle her breast. Bernard stood speechless.
'Maude,' said Bernard, 'we should call her Ivy, look how she clings.'

Maude smiled, 'Ivy shall be her name.'
'Ivy Maude Dixon,' spoke Bernard after a while.
Outside there was a clip clop of horses' hooves going down the winding path.
'That's dad on his early morning round,' said Maude
'It looks as though he will get busier as time goes on,' Bernard remarked.
Bernard watched his new-born daughter suckling at her mother's breast.

Several weeks later as they all sat around the evening fire Pops said, 'Bernard, we would like you to be a full partner in the firm of Boothroyds Coal Merchants. We can change the name to Boothroyd and Dixon.'
Bernard looked at the fire blazing, then looked at Pops. His face went red then white with shock. He sat quietly. Pops knew Bernard would not answer straight away.
'Maude, did you hear that,' Bernard said, 'your dad just asked me if I want to be a partner. I'll not turn it down,' he told them.
'Good for you Bernard,' Maude said.
The day after Ivy Maude Dixon was christened, documents were signed legally and binding in Campbell and Campbell Solicitors' Office. Boothroyd and Dixon were partners.
'To Boothroyd and Dixon, may we have many successful years to come,' said Pops raising his glass in the air. 'Another surprise lad,' said Pops. 'We want you, Maude and Ivy to take over the second floor of this house, isn't that right Mother.'
'Yes,' she said with a toothless grin.
Bernard and Maude looked at each other with surprise.
'To happy families,' said Pops. As everyone raised their glass.
'You do know Pops,' said Bernard 'one day I will want to build Maude our own house on the piece of land I bought several years ago.'
'I know lad, until then we will enjoy the happy noise of children running through this house, even if it's for only a short time. Isn't that right Mother?' Pops called out.

A year and seventeen days later, Maude gave birth to another girl. Everyone was delighted
'A sister for Ivy,' announced Bernard.
'What will her name be,' asked Pops.

'She is pure as a white lily,' said Bernard. 'Lilly Martha Dixon.'
Martha Boothroyd was delighted and tears slowly slid down her tired face.

One Friday morning as Bernard and Pops went past the market stalls in Little Hamblyn, they noticed several children with placards around their necks. Pops pulled the horses to a standstill and stared.
'I've never seen ought like this before lad, have you.' said Pops to Bernard.
'No,' answered Bernard, 'it's a hard life in that house hold for sure.'
'We could do with someone to look after these horses Bernard,' said Pops.
'Aye,' said Bernard in agreement.
'Come on lad, let's go over and have a look,' said Pops climbing down from the cart.
They walked slowly over to where several ragged boys stood.
'What's your name,' asked Pops. 'Are you all related?
The boys nodded their heads. They were underfed, dirty and looked bewildered.
'Where's your mother,' asked Bernard.
'Dead,' said the oldest.
More people began to gather round them.
'I can only take one of yer, said Pops.
Pops and Bernard looked hard at them.
'What's year name lad,' asked Pops to the second youngest.
'Tommy, he said quickly. 'Where's yer Dad,' asked Bernard.
'Dead,' they all said together.
There was a gasp of horror from the gathered crowd.
'You can come with us Tommy,' said Pops. 'Every Sunday you can have off to meet up with yer brothers.'
Within five minutes all boys were taken in with the same promise. Boothroyd and Dixon took on little Tommy Stack to tend the stables for them. They made him a room over the top of the stable where he could sleep.

A year later Bernard noticed Pops was getting slower with carrying the sacks of coal. He would have a word with everyone the next Sunday evening. Bernard spoke to Tommy first before he left to meet his brothers.

'How would you feel Tommy on becoming a coal delivery boy?'
Tommy nodded his head. 'Aye Mr Dixon.'
The following Saturday afternoon Bernard went into the stables as usual to check all was clean and tidy.
'Do you feel strong enough Tommy in carrying the sacks of coal on your shoulders,' asked Bernard.
'Aye Mr Dixon, I've been practising for a long time now,' said Tommy.
'Are you happy Tommy, asked Bernard.
'Aye Mr Dixon,' said Tommy.
'I know it's a hard life for you and your brothers being apart,' said Bernard.
Sunday evening everyone sat round the open fire.
'Pops, I think it's time for you to stop humping the sacks of coal,' said Bernard looking across at the old man's tired face.
'Who will help you Bernard,' asked Pops.
'Tommy,' said Bernard.
Pops nodded his head in agreement.
'Well I can help in the stable,' said Pops.

Two years later Maude gave birth to another daughter. Bernard and Maude sat looking at her in the crib.
'She's a quiet one,' said Bernard. 'There's nothing wrong with her is there?'
'No,' said Maude, 'she is content, and we still have not given her a name.'
'Rose,' said Bernard. 'Rose Mary Dixon.'
Today was Ivy's first day of school in the village hall. Maude held Ivy's hand as they went down the winding path. In the schoolyard children were playing. Maude knew the first day of letting go would be the hardest. It was a hard life at times with so much to do.

Inside the classroom, the wooden desks stood in rows. Miss Wilson, the miller's daughter, showed Ivy to hers. She sat down at her desk, looked at her mother with a large smile on her rosy face. With a tear in her eye Maude left.

There was a clip clop of horses' hooves. Ivy's eyes widened.
'That's Sonny and Jim,' Ivy said excitedly.
Miss Wilson smiled. She knew how she felt.

Bernard watched Pops as he struggled to carry the last bag of coal on his shoulders inside the shed. He would definitely have a word with him tonight.

Bernard spoke with Tommy on arriving back into the stables.
'Tommy, Pops won't be coming out again, don't let him argue with you.'
Tommy nodded his head.
'These odd days he comes out are no good to you either Tommy, so stand your ground.'

After evening meal, Maude put the children to bed, Bernard spoke out.
'Pops, I do not want you coming out again. It's Tommy's job now. You're too old and I will not be responsible for you.'
'We're partners,' his father-in-law said.
'Yes, and you're a sleeping partner,' said Bernard. 'Enough is enough. Tell him Ma.'
Pops looked at his wife; she glanced up at his face.
'You know the stables are too much for you.'
Bernard glanced at Tommy, who nodded his head in agreement.
'Next week, we look for a stable boy,' said Bernard.

RECLAMATION

Anita Richards

'Why do you want to go to Wicken?'
'Because I do,' I smiled in a way I hoped was enigmatic.
I wanted to look at a house I once knew. Or rather, a house I didn't get to know. How I didn't get to know you. I twiddled the bracelet on my wrist.
'Is that new?'
'No. I just haven't worn it for a long time.'
'You have got it bad. this wanting to return to the past. It's like wanting to return to the womb.'
Funny. I had always thought of the house as a tomb. Maybe unfulfilled womb was more appropriate.

He drove in silence. The sound of silence used to fill the house in every nook and cranny. Yes, like the empty womb waiting for the baby never to be nurtured there, never to be born. Like our marriage. There had been the conception, but no nurturing into life. You had spent every penny on the house that started as a bungalow, but for us didn't become a home. The idea had been for rooms to fill the space in the roof - as and when - only as and when didn't happen. Anyway the builder reckoned it would be less expensive to complete the house in one stage. 'With enough power points in each room for twin beds.' Goodness, what did you expect, a football team?

Once built there were many empty rooms. Furniture was sparse, the wood block floor required polishing on hands and knees while the stairs remained uncarpeted. There were no luxuries for life in the country in the Sixties, like a washing machine which unlike today wasn't an every day item but when your husband is a veterinary surgeon, a necessity. All the trousers, shirts and vests caked with blood and cow dung that was emitted in fear during labour, as you inserted your arm beyond the elbow trying to feel within the uterus, that I washed by hand.

But it had its moments. When I could be with you watching as a live calf dropped onto the straw with a squelch and a thud and a soft bellow from Mother, who turned to nuzzle her new-born with encouragement for the struggling legs and tiny feet to gather themselves together into a new form, a new life, to search for and reach the heavy laden teat upon which survival depended. The gentle moo moo of the mother, as the tiny mouth, lips gathered, began to suckle. The ecstatic joy of mother and infant bonding was overwhelming and wonderful.

But the occasions of live calves being extricated from the depths were less usual than the cow bellowing in the agony of unrequited pregnancy. These call outs showed the blood and pain of unrewarded labours. When cows go literally mad as their dead offspring are dragged away. I only hope these days, psychology is allowed to play its part and the bereaved mothers at least allowed to nose their babies, so they can acknowledge the existence of their still born offspring and know the hormonal disturbance and labour was not a fantasy, even though they may have been regarded as just a machine to produce milk. For veterinary intervention was usually left too late to save the calf, or indeed sometimes the mother. The farmer's main concern it seemed to me, was preserving finances rather than preservation of Life.

I thought of the night you woke me at 2am to go with you to a gypsy camp when the gods smiled in your favour, as a pony struggled in labour in the middle of the night. Your boss usually kept such auspicious happenings for himself. It was magical. The old type Romany caravan, the kettle boiling over the spitting flames and a live foal at the end of a hard night's labour for mare, infant and vet alike. The drive home as dawn broke, the sky shot with blues and mauves, as the stars sparkled and disappeared to accompany the moon to the other side of the planet. The sort of night, where in novels, one gets home and becomes pregnant from the ecstasy of sharing such an experience.

With hindsight I realise you knew me better than I thought. You nearly brought me home a calf to hand rear, whose mother had died. But you decided against it. You knew I would never give him up when the time came. How right you were. As indeed when you refused my desire to become carer to a German Shepherd, saying 'Any dog you have will be boss, with those you have to be their boss'. Wise words David, although I resented them at the time.

He braked. 'Come on, which way now?'

'Oh sorry, I was miles away.'

'I told you revisiting the past is not a good idea.'

I sighed. 'If you head along the main road here, then turn left, just before leaving the village.'

The day we moved in was chaos. The workmen were still sanding the floor. It was the day before our first wedding anniversary, and the only time you bought me flowers. Red carnations. My mother looked at my father when she saw them saying I wouldn't want the bunch of pink pyrethrum they had brought. Such a sad thought. I can only love them more with an understanding of their sadness. My beagle sat on my knee in the grey Volkswagen as we pulled up outside. Maybe you should have carried me over the threshold.

'You're away again. When I turn left, then what?'
'There's a bungalow, a side road, then the house opposite an open field.'

I had expected the geography to stay the same. How naive. I hadn't reckoned for the time lapse. For change. For moving into the New Millennium.

The field that had proclaimed the changing seasons, from the drilling of the dark earth, the setting of the corn, the fresh greenness and the fulfilment of golden harvest, the old Dutch barn standing in the corner, the piles of fresh manure that had scented the air, had disappeared. The overhead cables were no longer a peaceful safe sanctuary welcoming the arrival and blessing the departure of the swifts, swallows and martins. What had been a quiet isolated country lane was now part of the commuter belt.
'Can you stop?' He pulled over to the left.

The house hadn't changed much from the outside, apart from the porch now enclosing the front door, and security light. The lawn, velvet smooth, with the lines of a freshly mowed cricket pitch, was empty. The rose bed had gone, the rose bush you planted for me. Tall evergreens you planned one day would glow with Christmas lights for the children that had remained unborn, were also gone. An MG sat outside the double garage, the door of which I had pulled down onto my head once in my eagerness to greet you after a long day alone and when you came home were too tired for conversation.

Until the phone rang, that is, and you were off on another call.

I thought of walking across the lawn with my mother, my parents' border collie, Mac, who had greeted me outside the church on my wedding day, leaving muddy pawprints over the train of my white dress, and my beagle, Bengy, my baby. Both dogs ran into the road as a car drove toward the Fen. I was never sure why, as I lunged forward, unable to reach them both, I choose to grab Mac, watching in horror as my beagle was rolled over by the car. Mercifully, probably saved by his thickened waistline, he straightaway stood up and barked disapproval at the now stopped vehicle. Of course, I should have called you but didn't. That's how I was in those days.

I waited, longing for your return to check my dog's health. He was a Christmas present in the first year of our marriage.

You had chosen him when he was three days old, when you clipped his dew claws, along with the rest of the litter. I guess I waited as excited as any mum-to-be for the six weeks to pass before he was weaned and came to our home and I prepared his baby-food formula. I pictured the back garden where one day we were to have a stable and horses.

I thought of the furniture and the shades of green, the grounded earth colours in curtains that I made for the eyes to the soul of the house, for the windows were large to let in the country air and views of the amazing cloud formations, the sometimes eerie daylight of flat Fens, the silver twinkling stars and moonglow of night. The stillness being occasionally pierced by the screech of an owl or the bark of a far off fox. I thought of the little vole who walked over your face one night, and the appalling lack of compassion and hypocrisy shown in this taker of the Hippocratic Oath, as you annihilated it by jumping on the tiny mammal.

I remembered the Fen blow when everything indoors and out was covered with the heavy black dust of Fenland soil. I remembered the slate fireplace with the coloured stonework, repeated on the outside by the front door. The smell and the sound of a coal fire. The sort in which we all watch pictures of our dreams born before they die, in the licking, flickering flames. I could even remember my clothes.
I recalled the family gatherings and the one and only visit to the village pub. The walks down the Fen, seeing specially bred swallow-tail butterflies, endangered even then, released into the wild, and searching

for the wild orchid, a favourite with my mother. The flood gates were opened as the locks closed in an attempt at denial, were swept away.

I remembered . . .

'Let's look round the Fen while we're here,' said my friend.

The pig sties were no longer at the end of the road that led into the Fen toward the windmill. The pigman once said he had bought his wife flowers for Mother's Day, although they had no children. 'She'll have to be a mother first,' you said looking at me. I never was. I remembered the pain, the despair and the aloneness. But the house had been built for us. You had cared, even loved me in your way. You had watched me walk down the aisle toward you, where I had outdatedly promised to obey. I had cared for you, even loved you, but my defences were such, I could never have known. Not then.
'Can we go now please?'
'Pilgrimage over?'
Before driving off, he hugged me.

In a day or two I would try to explain what I had been doing was not to wallow in the mud caused by tears of the past. I wasn't trying to relive any of this. What I have done in my life is try to write it off. Self-annihilation by deceit. A kind of living suicide. Trying to convince myself of my awfulness and pretend that life hasn't happened. I had thrown all photographs away but luckily one of the few remaining relatives had been able to give me one of my wedding day. My parents looked good that day, looked proud of their only child, who unites their union throughout time.

I thought about beginnings. I thought about birth. How the experience is more traumatic for some. When you die to the tranquillity or the turmoil of the womb and enter into life. When you are thrust from the comforting warmth of Mother's body into the cold space that should be filled with the warmth of maternal love, so our worth and our self-esteem are not in question. It wasn't my mother's fault, or my father's, although he preferred to accept blame. Nor was it mine for that matter. But the way it was at my birth led me to believe the death of anyone or anything I love was my fault. That separation at birth seemed to mean death, not the beginning of life. It was deeply ingrained into my unconsciousness and the unconscious choices subsequently made.

I had wanted this journey to end my denial of life. The denial of having been loved and having loved in the past. I wanted to regain memories that contained an acceptance of life. I hadn't tried to relive the past nor to bury it. My desire was reclamation. To reclaim my past. For some of who I am today is because of those who have been in my life. To allow myself to know I have a past, rich and impoverished, like most. I think I had tried to hate you for loving me because of low self-esteem nurtured by parents unable to claim their own worth. To accept that I have been loved and have loved.

Hopefully with this acceptance will come the knowledge that maybe, one day, I will love and be loved again.

Reprise

Michael Davidson

Sitting quietly in a train for Liverpool one morning, I suddenly realised a lady of huge proportions was approaching, carrying a shoulder bag the size of a holdall, while a porter, one quarter her size was pushing her two enormous suitcases on a trolley.
'Ah, here it is. My carriage. Now I must find my reserved seat.'

Breathless and anxious, she heaved herself into the carriage while the porter lifted the suitcases on to the luggage rack. She fumbled in her handbag for a tip and expressed her thanks with a quick smile.

She was certainly in her fifties but her chubby, young-looking face belied this. She wore a well-cut grey suit, a sensible blouse and matching shoes. Neatly trimmed wisps of grey hair just showed beneath her broad-brimmed hat which circled her nervous-looking face.

As she put her shoulder bag in the corner seat, the train jolted slightly but it was enough to topple her on to her bag. I attempted to assist.
'Thank you. They could have waited another moment. If only my alarm clock hadn't failed me,' she said, as if it was all my fault.
'Never mind,' I said, 'you still caught the train.'
'That's as maybe,' she said, 'unfortunately I had no time for breakfast this morning and I'm absolutely gasping for a cup of tea - I *am* so thirsty. I'm going to pop along to the buffet and see what I can find.'

Again, with unseemly haste she squeezed her way into and along the corridor. Had she arrived earlier, she would have learnt from the apologetic announcement that the system supplying hot refreshments had broken down and there was some doubt if repairs could be completed in time. Soon I heard her remonstrating with an unlucky official. She was quite florid when she returned.
'Guess what?' she divulged. 'There's no tea at all. Can you believe it? It's all broken down. They're full of apologies - but no tea.'
'Oh dear,' I said, feigning astonishment. 'perhaps there's a soft drink.'
'I can't take acidity first thing in the morning. And I *am* so thirsty. What am I going to do? I shall die! Oh that wretched alarm clock - of all days!'

'When we get to Crewe,' I said, trying to soothe her, 'you will have time to get your tea there, but for now I'm afraid we'll just have to accept the inconvenience.'
'Inconvenience!' she boomed. 'It's a catastrophe. No tea, just think of it.'
'There are worse things,' I suggested.
'I must say you seem to be taking all this very philosophically.'
'It happens that tea is not to my taste. Very occasionally black coffee. Don't worry, after all we survived the war . . . '
'That's what everybody says,' she interrupted, 'but there's no war now.'
'We'll survive this, I assure you.'
'How?' she said. 'I *am* so thirsty. What shall I feel and look like at the fashion house without a cup of tea is unthinkable. Where are you going to, if I may ask?'
'As it happens I'm a marketing manager on my way to impress a business seminar and my station is way beyond Crewe - Chester,' I said with pointed emphasis.
She tried to look sympathetic. 'Mine's even further - Liverpool.'
'Meanwhile,' I suggested tactfully, 'it's rather important I catch up with my reading.'
'Reading! No, don't tell me - yes I have - I've left my book behind. Just when it was getting exciting. No I haven't. I know, it's in the blue case. I know where I put things. B for blue, B for books. Oh dear,' she said, as she rose.
'Allow me,' I said.
'You really are very kind. What would I do without you?'
'Be deprived of your literature,' I suggested.

With the balancing act of a juggler and the strength of an ox, I got her blue case down, just preventing it from bouncing off the seat.
'Thank you so much,' she said, and immediately set to work.

Strap after strap was unbuckled, keys were turned in what appeared to be security locks, then the case was ready to be unzipped.
'If only I'd packed a vacuum flask,' she sighed, 'but I hadn't time. Oh I *am* so thirsty.'

She poked around until she found the book. Straps were buckled, keys were turned and the case was zipped up again.

'Let's leave the case, I really mustn't trouble you again,' she said.

She began to read but soon fell asleep. After nearly two hours, an announcement that we were approaching a station woke her. She could hardly believe her ears.
'Is it true?' she said, jumping up excitedly.
'It certainly is,' I said. 'An unscheduled stop.'
'Oh, tea! What marvellous news.'

She plunged out of the train and joined a small queue. Within a few minutes she was yelling.
'My handbag! My handbag!' and rushed towards the carriage.

For a moment I thought she had been robbed.
'I've forgotten my handbag.'
'Here,' I said and quickly gave her what loose money I had in my pocket. She rejoined the queue like lightning.

After a few more minutes, I could see she was nearing the tea van and just as suddenly the whistle blew.
'Oh no!' she said. 'Please.'
A more disconsolate sight walking back to the train you could never see.
'Once again, no tea,' she said.
'I'm afraid so,' I said, helping her in.
'Thank you. I'm always forgetting something. Your money.'

I tried to cheer her up, saying that the train would be in Crewe in about an hour. She looked at her book, read a little, lay back in her seat and dozed, only to be disturbed by the ticket collector.
'What's happened?' she blurted out. 'Oh, it's you. Now where did I put my ticket? Don't tell me I dropped it at the last station. That really would be the limit. No tea, no ticket.'
She hunted everywhere, emptying the contents of her handbag on the seat. The ticket collector waited patiently, obviously used to seeing what handbags contained.
'It must be somewhere,' she said.
'I'm sure you'll find it, madam,' said the ticket collector, about to move to another passenger.
Fortunately, I happened to spot it in her book.

'Isn't that it?' I said with some relief.
'Silly me,' she said. 'I forgot all about it - thank you. I'm so sorry. What's the page? Thirty.'
'Thank you madam,' said the collector, courteously.
She refilled her handbag except for a small photograph.
'My nephew,' she said proudly.
'He appears to have a mind of his own,' I said, after a quick look.
'He certainly does,' the lady said, emphatically.
She then proceeded to praise his academic skills beyond belief and I was inundated with so many statistics, I could take in little and remember even less. Finally, she gleefully told me he was top of his form at school and had earned the captaincy of the cricket team.
'First eleven,' she stressed. 'The Hutton of Halliwell he's called. Made a century last week, or was it half a century? Anyway, I know he got more runs than anyone else. Everyone was astonished but I knew he'd do well. They don't know him as I do. He'll certainly have no difficulty making something of himself in this world, you'll see. He's made his mark already. He knows exactly what he's going to do. Play cricket for England, after university of course. And I know what I must do - beauty sleep and then some reading.'
'I think I might do the same,' I said.
'You did say you were going to catch up on your reading - I do hope I haven't prevented you.'
'Not at all. I'll have plenty of time after a rest,' I said. And with that I tried to settle down to a well needed sleep.

In my dream I saw this lady at a fashion show drinking tea out of an endless number of silver cups which were then presented to her nephew. Each time I stirred, I could see a heaving mass fast asleep. The next time I stirred, I heard the ticket collector announcing that we would be stopping at Crewe for fifteen minutes. As I opened my eyes, there the lady was, nose powdered, hat adjusted, dress straightened, handbag on her arm, marching out of the train as if she were about to take the salute on a parade ground.
'I *am* so thirsty,' she exclaimed in a way which indicated her ordeal would soon be over.

Within five minutes, she emerged from the buffet beaming with delight. Holding two plastic cups, she said gleefully, 'My second, and this is for you - black coffee.'

'That's very thoughtful of you,' I said, taking the two cups from her as she clambered aboard.

'You'll be Marketing Director yet,' she said as she sat down, happily sipping her tea.

'And you'll be Director of your fashion house,' I ventured.

She chuckled. When she had finished her tea, she lay back on the seat completely relaxed, a picture of absolute contentment. Somehow she didn't look quite so large and years younger. As I was thinking how kind she had been, her eyes began to close and I hoped that there would be no more wailing. Within a matter of seconds, a voice whispered sleepily, 'Oh! I *was* so thirsty, I *was* so thirsty' - at fairly regular intervals all the way to Chester.

I Close My Eyes

Kate Attfield

They came out of nowhere. They came out of nothing. The white walls couldn't keep them in and they wouldn't be kept out; that's why the room was abandoned.

The floor is bare, save an empty bed in the corner and the dust settling on every surface each day like a new skin. The room isn't dark; that isn't why it feels so ominous. There's a lot of light in the room because all that covers the large windows are two white bedsheets, stapled to the ceiling. Maybe if the sheets weren't there, but some thick, black curtains making sure the light couldn't get in, you wouldn't see the room and it wouldn't feel so strange. So empty, but so claustrophobic at the same time.

You could put someone terrified of spiders in that room now and wait, and wait, and sooner or later they'd wish for even the nastiest looking arachnid to crawl towards them and keep them company.

There's nothing in that room, nothing you can see but something, *somethings*, you can feel, somethings you know are watching you, waiting for you to turn your back, to go to sleep. That's why the room was abandoned.

She scratched her way along the wall. She could feel the mud or muck or slime, whatever it was beneath her hands and the rough stone under that, but she didn't care. She still didn't care when a jagged piece of stone that was jutting out from the wall stabbed at her hand, shooting pain up her arm. At least she could feel her way along.

There was no light. There was no air, no movement around her to let her know where she was. There was only the terrible stillness and the shrieking, the screaming which was so high-pitched sometimes that she thought her ears would bleed, which was so loud she thought *they* were right on top of her . . . but they never were right on top of her, they were always just behind her, just reaching for her, just touching her shoulder . . .

She sat upright and caught the breath in her throat. She coughed, choked trying to get the air into her lungs. 'Don't panic!' she told herself, 'They're not real,' she said, but at the same time she glanced down at her hands.

A long, painful sob echoed around the room and disappeared as soon as it had appeared as she threw her head down into the covers, which were tucked around her shaking body. She tried to choke the sound away, to keep still, to pretend that it was alright. It was the same sound she made every night when she woke up with tears in her eyes, her breath choking her as she sat up so suddenly. They were the same covers that she plunged her face into to make sure she couldn't be heard, and they were the same slimy stains on her hands that were always there when she woke up from feeling her way along the wall in the blackness, asleep.

She lifted her head again, the weariness already trying to pull her down into unconsciousness, and examined her hands. The slime *was* there. She wiped them on the covers, over and over, trying to get them clean, get rid of the horrible shiny scum, her body shuddering like thunder as the sobs came out silently. Tears blurred her vision as she looked at her hands again. 'Please don't let it be real, please . . . ' Her
hands were clean now. This meant she could, once again, happily convince herself that maybe she was going crazy, that the creatures, the monsters, weren't really there when she closed her eyes, and she could be calm.

A small, relieved smile started to tremble on her lips as she found the thought of madness a comfort to the alternative, the only thing she could do to try and stop her fear. It flickered momentarily, and froze in a grimace, a display of horror as she watched, small at first, a patch of blood grow and dribble down her hand and onto the slimy bedcovers. Why was she bleeding? There had never been blood before! Her breath stopped. Her body trembled again and she remembered catching her hand on the wall, in the black, in her dream.

How could there be blood? She had been asleep, it was a dream, a nightmare. But nightmares weren't real, they didn't exist, you only had to open your eyes and they were gone. They couldn't hurt you, could they? But there was nothing else to cut herself on. She'd made sure there was nothing else. There was only a bed. A room with a bed and a door, and even the door had been nailed shut from the inside. Nothing could get in, nothing!

The rest of the night passed turbulently into the day, which passed slowly and uncertainly. It was like every other day. She crouched in the corner of the bed with covers wrapped around her shoulders, her face peering around the sheet hanging across the window. She would see some people pass in the street below her, would hide if they happened to glance up and see her. She didn't know why she hid from them, she wanted to scream out to them, 'Help!' She wished someone could hear her pleading for help, but they never did because she never spoke. If she had spoken, if they had ever heard her, would they do anything anyway? Would they believe her? Did they all have nightmares like she did?

She couldn't remember when they started, she couldn't remember anything after they started. She found it hard to remember anything at all anymore. She'd forgotten her name now.

All she could do was sit as still as she could and as quietly as she could and wait for the night, try not to fall asleep. She would try not to fall asleep all night as well but she knew she would, she always did. They controlled her now, controlled what she did and where she went. She didn't know why she'd nailed the door closed - she didn't know where she'd got the nails or that she'd had a hammer or where it was now. She didn't know when she'd last been outside and breathed the fresh air, not the dank, stale air in the room lulling her back into the nightmares.

Night came again. Stay awake, stay awake, don't close your eyes. Please don't . close . . your . . . eyes . . . . Everything was black again but she wasn't where she had been before. She couldn't feel the wall alongside her now, couldn't feel the moisture in the air, radiating from the horrible but familiar wall. She couldn't hear the shrieking.

She moved backwards, step by step. Something hard hit her back on either side. A corner, she was in the corner of the darkness. She squinted her eyes, tried to focus on something. A shape. There was something, a shadow, a movement . . . a glint of eyes, teeth? She dropped down into the corner quickly, drew her knees up to her chin trying to make herself as small as possible. If she was tiny maybe they wouldn't see her. A tear ran down her cheek and she began to shake.

The shrieks came. They were everywhere but not distant now, so close. Not behind her now, but in front, right in front of her. There wasn't stillness now, they were moving, they were circling. The shrieking was different as well. Before they had been chasing. They had stopped chasing now, they had caught now. They were laughing. Inhuman. Screaming. Piercing. Dreadful. Laughing. Her ears felt cold, felt wet as if the bloodcurdling sounds were running down into her head. She wrapped her hands around her head quickly, before the noise got in.

A warm, damp breeze on her cheek nearly stopped her heart. Another breeze and another, only they weren't breezes, they were too controlled, they were breaths, it was breathing. A small, soft sound escaped from her lips as she felt the oozing skin close to hers. A screech rose from the darkness. Another and another. She felt her terror rip through her until she could no longer control her body. She felt wet run down her legs, puddling on the floor. The shrieks became enraptured.

She stood quickly and felt *it* rise after her, felt it reach towards her, still screaming, touch her neck, her cheek, scrape her skin - pain as the claws reached inside her cheek. Blood burst out of her face.

The bed was soaked, the covers were strewn about the room. The bed sheets hanging down limp, as they always did. The dust hadn't been disturbed on the floor. Small specks of brown sprayed on the covers. Large patches of slimy residue, wiped there.

It was puzzling to everyone. The door nailed shut from the inside. The windows bolted down tight, curtains hanging limp, no holes in the walls anywhere, but the room, empty, nonetheless.

What was worse was the knowledge that someone, the tenant, a young girl they had to assume, had died in that room. The bloodstains in the corner couldn't be ignored. There was not enough blood there to suggest that the person had died there, but the manner in which it was spread over the walls, the hand-prints, the nail marks - so frantic that they had driven the blood deep inside the wall surface - there was something terrifying about it all.

They found nothing in the room but the blood and the bed and the makeshift curtains. They found scratches from something, near the bloody prints in the corner, but no one could be sure what they were.

So the room is empty again. The walls have been freshly covered over in white so you can't see the stains. A fresh coat of varnish has been put down on the floorboards and decent curtains have replaced the bed sheets. The room looks warm now, but it doesn't feel warm. A room should have personality, people say. This room hasn't got a nice one and strangely enough, all I want to do in it is sleep.

Holly And The Psychic-Line Lady

Cliff De Meza

As Holly awoke, she was aware of the bright sunlight shining through the pretty flowery curtains which hung at her east facing bedroom window. She turned restlessly and yawned, then got up and drew back the curtains. What a beautiful day greeted her. She opened the window wide and breathed in the fresh morning air, the smell of the honeysuckle in the front garden wafted up towards her. The Postman in his bright uniform was just getting into his little red van. 'Nice morning Holly,' he called. Holly just giggled. He was a cheeky Postman, and knew everyone and everything in their small village community of East Cunforth. She realised that she was the first one up on this Saturday morning, and she skipped downstairs to get the post. Most of it was letters and bills connected with her dad's plumbing business, and a letter for her mum from Auntie Flo. She only lived in West Cunforth the next village, but without a phone or a car she relied on the family to take her shopping at the superstore, and run other errands for her. She was a nuisance at times, and was also very nosy. 'What does she want now?' murmured Holly to herself as she fingered her long blonde hair.

Just then the letterbox clattered, and through came the local weekend paper. It was published in the nearby market town, where Holly was at college learning hairdressing. She found it usually had little of interest in it, but today would be different. As she picked up the paper it had half unrolled, and the bottom half of the front page was facing her. There he was staring at her from the front page: It was him! The one love of her young life! The boy her mother had forbidden her to see since they used to go to the pictures together when she was 12 and he was 14. There he was in his red and white football strip; a broad smile on his face; a football tucked under his left arm, and in his right hand a silver challenge cup. 'How handsome he is now!' thought Holly as her feelings started to bubble over, and she wondered if she would dare to phone him. She almost swooned in a moment of fantasy, then she turned over the paper and her eyes fell on the headline above the article. '*Local Sportsman Killed In Biking Tragedy!* End of promising career for 20 year old Jason Briggs of West Cunforth.'

Holly screamed, and collapsed onto the hall floor. Her mother came running downstairs, and picking up the paper immediately realised the cause of her daughter's distress, but reacted very inappropriately. 'Oh how dreadful! We knew him didn't we - at one time. You used to go to school with him, do you remember Holly?' How stupid can parents get? Is it something they learn, or does it come naturally? Holly with tears streaming down her face, and her mother sipped black coffee as they read the account of the tragic accident. Jason's new motorbike had skidded on a wet road near his home, and hit a tree.

Next Auntie Flo's letter was opened, and as expected it contained a graphic account of the accident, though quite different from the official one in the press. Predictably it concluded 'Good riddance to bad rubbish I say. That family never were any good. I knew I did the best thing to tell you about them and insist that you stopped Holly seeing that boy, when they were at school. Courting at that age. Disgusting. Wouldn't have been allowed in my day.' Auntie Flo did have a certain way with words.

By now Holly's dad had come down, and had made himself aware of the problems. He cradled Holly in his arms, as only a father can do. 'I always thought he was a nice lad. We used to support the same team in those days you know.' His wife glowered at him across the kitchen, still holding Auntie Flo's damming letter in her hand. 'Did I tell you I met him the other week?', continued her father. 'When I went with your Uncle Bert to that cup match. He remembered me and asked after you. I told him you were learning to be a hairdresser. Lovely lad! I wish you'd kept up with him. Come to think of it, he did ask if you had a boyfriend.' His wife stormed out of the kitchen, slamming the door behind him.

Holly was now in floods of tears again, and that continued from time to time throughout the day. That evening, as was their custom after watching the match on TV, her parents set off to the local pub for a meal. Usually Holly would have her friend Caren round to watch videos or listen to CD's but Caren was on holiday with her parents this week, so she was home alone.

The grief: The anguish: How was she going to cope? If only she had been able to tell him she still loved him. Perhaps she still could, after all people say they go to Heaven, and people claim to communicate with the dead! She looked frantically through the paper. There it was a small advert inviting people to a service at the Spiritualist Church. Holly phoned the number: A kindly man listened patiently to her story and her request for a message to be sent to Jason beyond the grave; then he said. 'I'm afraid we can't help you my dear. You see you don't really understand. We get a lot of enquiries from bereaved people. It doesn't work like that. Perhaps you should be talking to the local vicar in your village, or a bereavement counselling organisation? I could give you their numbers.' Holly declined the offer, and disappointed put the phone down.

Then she caught sight of last Sunday's paper under the TV. Looking through the advert pages; desperate for help, advise, or even just someone to talk to now; she found a block advert in the personal column: 'Phone-a-Psychic. one-to-one private consultations. Only 60p per minute.' She dialled the number, and after only two rings a lady with a very posh voice answered. 'Thank you for calling 'Phone-a-Psychic'. My name is Madam Griselda. Please tell me your name and date of birth.'

I'm Holly,' she began in between the sobs and sniffs, 'and my date of birth is 9th January 1980.'

Madam Griselda quickly tapped on her pocket calculator, and established that her caller was 18 years old and therefore old enough to use the service. 'Holly, I'm a Tarot reader. First I'll do a general reading, while you think of specific questions to ask later. I'm shuffling the cards now; tell me when you want me to stop.'

That wasn't what Holly wanted, but she heard the shuffling of cards, as if they were deliberately held near the phone, then she sort of half sobbed 'Stop please.'

'Oh!' said the Psychic in a surprised voice, 'I see from the cards that you are very upset my dear. Perhaps you've had a row with someone close to you! - You're not pregnant are you? Has someone died!'

Holly couldn't answer, she just burst into floods of tears again. Eventually she blurted out, 'The only boy I ever loved has been killed on his motorbike. I want to tell him I love him. Perhaps if I kill myself I could be with him!'

All of a sudden the posh voice was gone, and a very matter of fact Yorkshire accent took over. 'I'm sorry I can't do this any more. Cum on luv, pull yourself together now. You need help, and I'm going to help you. Yu'v to phone me at home after 7, d'yer understand. I'll give you the number it's . . .' Holly recognised the code as being the Leeds area, her father dealt with suppliers from there, and she carefully wrote the number down on the margin of the Sunday paper. 'By the way me real name's Ann, I'm 27 and married. Me 'usband's out of work at moment, that's why I'm doing Tarot readings. You will phone me later luv won't you? Promise now! I will try and help you.' Holly agreed, and put the phone down.

'How strange,' thought Holly as she made herself a coffee and began to pick at the ham salad her mother had left for her tea. 'I will ring Ann, I will,' she told herself. She was beginning to feel better already. Perhaps this Ann could help her. Well it was about a quarter-past seven when she picked up the phone and dialled the Leeds number.

''ello,' said a pleasant man's voice.
'Oh!' began Holly. 'May I speak to Ann please?'
'Aye rite enough lass, 'oo is it?'
'It's Holly, Ann asked me to phone.'
''Olly for thee luv.' The man shouted over the noise of the TV in the background. There was a faint click, then another and the sound of the TV vanished.
'Holly. How are you luv, are you feeling a bit better now?' Ann's soothing tone immediately put Holly at her ease, and she agreed that she was feeling a lot better. 'Well I think you need someone to talk to dear, and that's something that I'm very good at. Before we talk about you. I'd better explain to you about me and the Tarot reading hadn't I?'

Holly agreed.

'Well, I haven't really got the gift. I'm a bit of a fraud really. I picked it up a bit from an old lady who lived next door to us when I was at school. Some of the kids used to think she was a witch, but I liked her. She was a lovely old dear.'

‘Sounds a bit like my Auntie Flo,’ said Holly. ‘She reads tea leaves at the village fete.’
They both started to giggle. The ice was broken. This was going to work.
‘Well,’ Ann went on, ‘I’m sure there are some very genuine psychics, but that phone line is a bit of a con. We are supposed to keep the clients as long on the expensive phone lines as we can. It’s not difficult to suss out people’s problems, most fall into well-known categories. I told you that you were very upset; well I knew that from the way you were blubbing into the phone.’
‘Oh yes, of course! Aren’t I silly?’ said Holly.
‘Not at all. You are typical, and that’s how it works. Anyway, I’ve quit now. I’m going to see the Manager of the supermarket where I used to work on Monday, to see if I can start back there again.’

‘Now then, what can I tell you about Tarot cards?’ continued Ann. ‘They date back to the Renaissance, and there are four suits: Swords - representing conflict, Wands - for work and competition, Pentacles or Coins - for marital affairs, and Cups - for emotions. The deck also includes Jacks, Naked Lovers cards and an Emperor card. It’s very revealing if done properly by an expert, and the accuracy can sometimes be quite uncanny.’
The two chatted on till nine o’clock. Here was a woman that Holly felt she could talk to, unlike her mother, her aunt or her snooty best friend Caren. They chatted a lot on the phone over the next few months.

Ann advised Holly to go to Jason’s funeral, which she did. Meeting up again with his parents and his older brother Mark, now 25 and joining his father’s law firm. It was not long before Mark was on the phone, asking Holly out on a date. They soon became ‘an item’, ‘courting’ as Auntie Flo would call it, and they married in the following spring. Why was it that Auntie Flo disliked the Briggs family so much? Perhaps she had read something in those tea leaves?

The Major's Roses

Harry Derx

It certainly was not just another day for the major. At least two important events were already scheduled in his diary. First in order of timing was the flower show. He had to have his roses booked in at the village hall by ten thirty in the morning. Then later in the afternoon was the actual show after the judging of the entries. As one of the leading lights of the village, this year he was not to be one of the judges because he was exhibiting himself. The other pleasant affair was the visit of his elder son from university up in Scotland, down for a weekend break. The major had not seen his son since his graduation with a degree nine months previously and had not met his fiancee, who was a student at the same university studying medicine.

Really, anyone who knew the major well would have known that no day was just another to him. He was one of those rare individuals who seemed never to have grown up. It was not that he sprang out of bed in the mornings like a two or three-year-old, eager and enthusiastic to enjoy the day's activities, but he did possess an exceptional energy and gift for living a full life.

This attitude to living was not of course to everyone's approval and at times was used by some to demean him. Nevertheless, it had brought him from a rather lowly and deprived childhood to a man of considerable status and respect. Such a person is naturally a perfectionist and this could never be denied.

With much care the retired army officer made his final selection from the rose bed in his garden. With all items to hand, he prepared the blooms for transit to the annual show. Because of the restricted entrance to the tiny car park at the village hall, he took his wife's smaller car to facilitate easier parking. As he drove off, he noticed she had left her digital camera lying on the back seat of the car. Making a mental note to remind her not to leave items lying around in the car, an afterthought occurred to him - yes, the camera could prove useful at the flower show.

It was a nice sunny Saturday morning, the roads were dry, though the previous day had been wet. Traffic was sparse, it not being a working day, but in his rear view mirror he saw a bright red sports car coming at a rate far in excess of the normal speed limits. Within seconds it sped past him and it was no surprise to notice the driver appeared to be a teenager. A couple of minutes later he reached the cross-roads where a right turn was the route to the village hall. Even while still a good distance away, he could see some obstacle in the roadway and approaching steadily, he was shocked to find a cyclist lying in the road beside a cycle lying on its side. Stopping the car he leapt out to the injured woman and was relieved to find her at least alive.

The victim of this mishap, a young woman, was badly shaken and bruised down the right side of her body, but having ascertained that no bones were broken, he assisted her to his car and moved the cycle to the grass verge. His acute observation noticed fresh tyre marks in the soft mud of the grass verge and the tree sapling that had been savagely smashed into. The young woman was able to tell him that the red car had given her a glancing blow, then skidded into the hedge on the right side of the road and quickly reversing, sped off.

It was obvious that the victim of this affair needed professional attention and sooner rather than later. The nearest hospital was about twenty minutes away, and that's where the major directed the car. He advised that she just rest and relax as much as possible during the journey to the casualty department. Arriving safely at the hospital, he left the injured person in the car and quickly summoned the medical staff to attend to her needs.

He gave the bare details as he knew them to the medics and having left his name and address, prepared to leave. Just as he was about to exit the front door, some remarks he overheard people in white coats discussing, about a young person believed to be high on drugs and the unlikely explanation for his condition registered in his mind. However, his main concern now was to get to the village hall as quickly as possible. Leaving the hospital car park, he noticed a red sports car with damage to the front bumper. He knew it was the same car he had seen earlier, so getting his wife's camera, he took a picture of it. Now it could be easily traced by the registration number.

On his return journey, as he approached the scene of the accident he saw a police car and two uniformed men examining the area at the corner. One of the officers signalled him to stop.

'What's the hurry?' he enquired, then recognising the major added, 'Oh, it's you sir.'
'I need to be at the village hall by ten thirty,' the major responded.
'Well you won't make that deadline, for it's nearly twenty to eleven now,' the constable said, showing his watch. 'There has been some kind of an incident here,' he continued, 'a damaged ladies cycle but no one seems to be around.'
'Well, as a matter of fact I can help you there,' the major volunteered. 'About three quarters of an hour ago on my way out, I saw a young woman lying in the road beside the cycle and I took her to Heston Hospital where I have just come from.'
'Was she badly hurt?' enquired the man in blue.
'I don't think so, but of course she was badly shaken up. She told me she was hit by a red car which then skidded into that corner of the grass verge by that small tree. The driver did not get out but just reversed and then carried on, and I am pretty certain I know that car.'
'Well what makes you believe you know which car was involved in this incident if you did not witness the event?' questioned the officer.
'Well, on my way from the Grange to the village hall where I was heading for, I was passed by a speeding red sports car that was doing at least a ton I think. It appeared to be driven by a teenager. At the hospital car park I saw a similar car with a damaged front bumper, in fact I have a photo of it in my wife's camera here in the car should it be needed.'
'Thank you major for your help to us and the unfortunate cyclist. Should you be needed elsewhere, I suggest you get going now.'

Frank Greenfield cut his rose blooms for the show. There was no doubt that they were quite spectacular as far as his usual roses went. But he now wished he had not challenged the major in the pub on Wednesday evening. He was not really a rose expert or even an enthusiastic gardener. It was just that putting some special fertiliser on them that his mother had bought at a boot sale had really given them a gigantic boost. His mother had suggested his entering the competition in the village hall. Even his sister, home for the weekend, had lent her encouragement for the escapade.

He got to the village hall at twenty-five past ten and was surprised to find the major not there. It was most unusual for the major to leave things to the last minute and the organisers were very strict as to the timing of the entries. While he was contemplating what possible cause could have prevented the major from participating in the show, his mobile phone rang. It was his mother ringing. She had received a message from the hospital that his sister, not badly injured, was being treated for an accident and would he call back home and ferry her over there.

Now Frank was doubly upset. If the major had no entry in the show, it would not be a fair victory for his to be declared the winner and there was five pounds at stake. This awkward situation, so unexpected at the last moment, left little time for careful, considerate and cool thought.

He made a decision and put his roses in the show, but in the major's name. He now returned home, picked up his mother and together they left for the hospital at Heston. At the junction of the cross-roads he saw a police car pull away and then he noticed the major about to drive off in his wife's car. He flashed his lights, to which the major responded, so he crossed over to pull alongside.
'Has the law finally caught up with you?' he called out.
'I have been doing my good deed for the day,' the major said, trying to hide his dejection.
'Shame you missed the flower show,' he called out, 'but I entered my blooms in your name.'
'Oh no, surely you did no such thing?' exclaimed the major. 'I simply cannot go along with that.'
'You probably would have won anyway,' Frank stated.
'No, no, it's positively unethical, I shall have to explain everything. What a terrible mess.' Now the major was upset.
'Look,' Frank urged, 'no one knows, anyone can take in an entrant's flowers.' He wanted to assure him it would pass unnoticed. 'Really, it might seem more suspicious if I won and you declining to exhibit. Where are your flowers anyway, they must outshine mine I am sure?'
'In this box,' said the major lifting the lid.
'Well, we are going to the hospital,' said Frank, 'we must get going.'
'Wait, if you are going to the hospital take these flowers, I know there is someone there they could cheer up.'
Frank was glad to get away. He was unsure what the major would do, what seemed a good idea could easily turn very sour indeed.

At the hospital his sister was very pleased to see her mother and brother. She had recovered quite a lot and was smiling broadly.
'How are you Hailey?' her mother enquired.
'I am a bit sore down the right side, but really I was very lucky things are not more serious,' she answered, then added 'they want to keep me here one night.'
'As these rose blooms could not be entered into the show,' Frank told his sister, 'I have brought them here to brighten up the place.'
'My, my, they are extra special. I am sure you could have won the competition outright. You should now consider entering the flower show every year,' she beamed.
To change the subject, Frank enquired, 'What time is your boyfriend expected to arrive?'
'His train should arrive at Heston station at 4pm, but he will go by taxi to the Grange to meet his father first.
Just then a nurse came in. 'What beautiful flowers,' she exclaimed. 'Aren't they champions?'

At the Grange the major was preparing to go to the village hall. He felt terribly uncomfortable over the way events had turned out. After considering all the factors and the additional trouble that sorting out the mess would entail, he decided to go along, whatever the outcome. Inside the hall he was approached by the chairman of the village club.
'I have to congratulate you and thank you, first for winning the rose competition, and secondly for your part in the return of my stolen car. The police informed me of your part in the matter and I am, of course, extremely grateful to have it back so soon.'
The major did not have to fake his surprise at this news, in fact the diversion of this new situation completely took away his feelings of guilt, allowing him to dismiss the other matter from his mind. He did not even go to look at the roses exhibited in his name.

Back at the Grange he merely told his wife that he had been successful at the village show. She told him that Arthur, his son, was having a shower and then they were going to visit his fiancee.
'And where exactly is his girlfriend?' the major asked.
'Well, she is not at home, but at the hospital. She phoned in a quarter of an hour ago.'

‘Ah indeed, of course, she is training for the medical profession. Perhaps she can’t keep away. I am keen to meet her, so let’s go.’ He fetched his car keys.

At the hospital the three of them were allowed in, though the rules stated a maximum of two visitors only. As soon as Hailey saw the major she said, ‘Thank you for being a good Samaritan this morning.’
‘Good Samaritan,’ his wife exclaimed, ‘What’s this all about? Tell me all the facts.’
Hailey relayed how she came off her cycle and how she got to the hospital.
‘I am really pleased you were around Dad,’ Arthur said.
‘I just happened to be in the right place at the right time,’ the major answered quietly.
‘Just look at those lovely roses. Aren’t they beauties?’ Arthur was pointing and really impressed.
‘Yes Frank, my brother, grew them,’ Hailey proudly said.
‘Well, how surprising,’ said the major’s wife.
‘They are so good, you could have grown them Dad,’ Arthur asserted.
‘Kind of you to say so,’ replied the major softly.

ISOBEL'S CANDLE

S R Fisher

The candle flickered, its dim orange light barely filling the corner of the room. My room. The curtains were open and I could see the silhouettes of the trees outside, along with a handful of stars and the large, full moon. I put on some sombre music and contemplated my next move. The candle, a gift from my friend Isobel, gently burnt itself to death. I reached carefully under my bed and produced my diary. I hadn't even so much as looked at it for almost a year. Yet tonight I felt an unbearable urge to write. I had something to say, and I couldn't move on until it was done.

I stared at the blank page, my pen between my teeth, and thought long and hard about where to begin. Over by the candle, a single, silvery object reflected in the light.

Since the accident, Isobel hadn't been to visit. Father told me that she came to see me at the hospital whilst I was unconscious, but I'm not sure if I believe him. As soon as I got home I tried to ring her. I knew she would be concerned, and I wanted to tell her that I could walk again, wanted her to see that I was on the mend and that everything was returning to normal. The phone rang, but there wasn't anyone home, and the answerphone was switched off. Disappointed, I put the phone down. I tried again two more times that night, still I didn't get an answer. It was only then that I realised she was on holiday.

Before the accident her parents had promised Isobel they would travel around Europe in the summer. She was probably sat on some warm, Italian beach by now. Isobel was always the lucky one. My father promised that we'd go on holiday, and yet every year we never did. Maybe next year Isobel's parents would let me join them. I've never been abroad before.

I had planned to keep the candle unlit, at least until Isobel got back from Europe, but I couldn't resist. I missed her, I had no one else to talk to. That candle was my only connection to her whilst she was away, so I lit it and watched its flame dance before me. It smelled of lavender, Isobel's favourite scent. Soon it would be gone, the wax melting in lines down the side of the candleholder.

Seven months ago, almost to the day, Isobel and I had gone shopping, we discovered a shop that day that we had never seen before. A little back street place filled with Celtic trinkets and books about dreams. They played strange, hypnotic music that sounded like a cross between a whale's call and the gentle lapping waves against a sandy shore. They also sold candles.

We would usually walk home. Today, for a change I thought we could take the bus. It was five minutes late and cost far too much, but we took it all the same. Isobel sat her three bags of clothes and little brown paper bag with candles in it beside her. She really loved her candles.

The bus made three stops before it was driven off the road by a car.

I don't remember which direction it came from, or even what colour it was, but I know I was pushed on top of Isobel and her shopping before everything went black.

I woke up three weeks later, unable to walk and barely able to speak. The doctors said it would be a while before I could leave the hospital, that I would need an operation on my legs, and that I would probably never walk again. But I proved them wrong.

As soon as I could I started using my legs. At first I could only move them up and down as I laid out on my bed, then the next stage was being able to sit up in the bed, rest my feet upon the floor and stand up. It took me two months to be able to do that. But I never gave up. After another three months I was walking by myself, or rather without the aid of someone holding me up. I still had my walking sticks. I doubt if I will ever get rid of them now.

Eventually the day came that I could check out of the hospital. My father came and picked me up, he drove very slowly and asked me if I was feeling any pain at least a dozen times on that short journey. God bless him.

Every day I checked the post, waiting for the postcard Isobel should have sent me. I've got a collection of them in my room, from all over the world. She always managed to fit everything she needed to say on the back of those postcards, and it was always a pleasure to read them.

It was like a fine art. She always began with 'It's beautiful here, you'd really like it . . . ' then go on to describe the location, how she'd spent her days and that she missed me.

I didn't get a postcard from Italy.

The hardest part about my life - since the accident - was trying to act as if nothing had happened. I went back to school, got bullied (but then, what's new?) and struggled to keep up with my studies. I even started to go out again at night. Usually Isobel and I would sit in the park, looking up at the stars and wishing our lives away. Now I sat there by myself. Isobel was having a very long holiday - she'd already missed the first three weeks of term, but I'd made an extra set of notes for her to have when she got back. I know she'd do the same for me.

So here we are, seven months since the accident, and I was alone. Isobel and her parents never came back. I'm not surprised they had decided to leave town - their work meant that they needed to travel a lot, and I suppose they just decided to live somewhere else. After all that's how Isobel ended up in this town in the first place. I shouldn't complain, wherever Isobel is, I'm sure she's better off. I just wish she would write to me, or phone me, anything to let me know how she's doing. She's probably got a new set of friends now. Friends that don't have scars across their face, friends that can go to the toilet properly, friends that aren't a burden.

For the first time in almost a year I'm here before my diary, a million thoughts swirling around in my head, and not a single one ready to put down on paper. I want to write something that describes how I feel right now, something that others can look at and know who I am. Understand what I must do. Something that Isobel can read one day, and see that I am sorry. It was my idea to go shopping that day. It was my idea to take the bus. It was all my fault.

It's time to put pen to paper. I hope I don't mess this up, like I have everything else.

Dear Diary
Has it only been seven months since I last spoke to you? It feels like so much more. I see the last thing I wrote was that I was going shopping with Isobel. Not a particularly special entry, yet in some ways it is the

most important thing I have ever written down. Since that day my life has stopped, crumbled into the earth, and been washed away by the coldest, icy rain the world has ever had the cruelty to make.

Once these pages were filled with humour, and childish gossip. Never again. When that car, its drunken driver passed out at the wheel, knocked my life over the edge and into the hands of God, so it stole my heart. Only my body returned that day.

Laid upon the hospital bed, a shattered eggshell of a person, I was lost to the world, wandering in an empty blackness. Somehow I never found my way out. Even if the doctors can heal a body, they cannot begin to piece together the mind, or the spirit. They remain shattered forever.

At first I did not want to concede to my frail, broken body. I took strength from deep within and started back upon the road to Normality. It was to be a journey that I could not complete.

I fear I am going mad. Or is this all a dream?

For a time I was happy. I had regained control of my body, and I thought that my heart had returned to me. Only to be torn out once more. There is a darkness where my happiness once was, an empty void filled with a guilt. A guilt I cannot bring myself to name, although it echoes throughout my blood.

I guess I truly am mad. And persecuted. For if this were a dream Isobel would be knocking on my door, choosing clothes for me to wear and ushering me towards the nearest shop. Yet I know that will never again happen. She has gone.

I am a walking corpse.

Help me.

As I sit here, my mind unsteady, I find myself considering an answer. I hear the words, now all I have to do is understand them.

My hands started shaking uncontrollably, and I could write nothing more. I looked down at what I had written. There, for the first time, I had put everything on paper. I had never written anything like it before.

I just hope that whoever finds it can understand. Though I doubt they ever will.

I blew out the candle and changed my pen for something else. Looking out at the shifting shadows beyond my window I finally found what I had been searching for all this time. There, dressed in the clothes she had bought that day seven months ago, was the name of my guilt. Isobel. She was hovering there, beckoning me to come closer. Her thin, white fingers waving slowly. I could do nothing but obey.

I felt the knife slide through my skin and pierce my breastbone. It touched my barely beating heart before my world went black once more. This time, with a tear in my eye, I chose not to return home.

THE LAST CHAPTER

Derrick Brain

The police constable eyed the tramp with disdain, to him such creatures were lazy beggars to be hurried off his manor. Jonathan Willetts looked at the constable with equal contempt. He did not care about his appearance. He did not care what people thought, neither did he care about the minor congestion his pram caused as he waived his way among the traffic and pedestrians of Croydon High Street.

Outside the central office block, Jonathan nimbly twisted his pram to block the entrance while he stepped into the office of Johnson and Taylor's Solicitors, two seconds ahead of the man in blue.

Two ladies conferring with each other behind a wide counter stared at the itinerant in dismay, it was Janet who beamed a welcome, 'Can I help you, Sir?'
'I got a letter.'

As Janet glanced at the letter she recognised what she had typed months earlier with her companion called Mr Taylor.

Nine years previously, Jonathan had walked out of the matrimonial home in a rage, now his thoughts created havoc in his mind. What senselessness possessed him, what evil spirit controlled him, was it bigotry which held him on the way of madness?
His musing was jerked back to the present by Janet asking, 'Would you like a cup of tea, Sir?'

When she produced a china cup and saucer with a plate of biscuits, he exclaimed, 'Real china from a real lady.'

Janet would have invited the constable to a cup of tea but Mr Taylor dismissed him with a curt, 'Mr Willetts is a client'. Mr Taylor was not concerned that some folk lived like tramps or that others as saints, the administration of wills was business. He obeyed the law, charged up a fee, added a little for profit and hoped for further work. In Jonathan's case, he hoped that business could be completed before another client entered the office.

'Your Aunt's estate has been wound up and all that remains is for us to settle with you.'
'If I refuse?'

Mr Taylor stared at his client and wanted to say 'You'd be a fool', instead he muttered 'There is no legal reason why not.' He noted Jonathan's head wobbled and added carelessly, 'You can now afford to live as a gentleman.' Instantly he regretted his words.

Jonathan's voice boomed round the room. 'I am a gentleman.'
It was Janet's calm, musical voice which eased the tension. 'A gentleman of the road, yes - a gentleman for God better.'

From a teenager Janet had been the member of a fundamental church while others of her age had gone overseas as missionaries or entered pastorates, her calling was a well kept secret.

Twice a month, dressed for a social evening, she caught a train to Victoria. On arrival she disappeared into the station cloakroom. When she emerged, the only clue to her identity was her sparkling blue eyes.

For two days and nights she helped man a soup kitchen, shared jokes with the homeless nomads, prostitutes and the mentally retarded. At that time she was asking herself, 'Is it worth it?' then a miracle, a tramp walked into the office as if to impress it on her mind. Ten minutes after he was gone a messenger brought a large box of chocolates, the greeting card read,
'The tea was lovely - love JW.'

As she offered Mr Taylor the box, she asked, 'What do you think of our latest client?'
'He needs a bath.'
'He had the freshness of country air upon him.'
'Mental.'
'Nothing with God is impossible - first find the cause.'
'Where do we start?' Mr Taylor emphasised the 'we', he could not help himself. The desire to be associated with Janet was just as deep as when she first entered the office seventeen years earlier.

'You could write to the brother.'
'If you write to him at the Embankment Mission.'

'Strictly official.'
'Yes - letters on file.'
Mr Taylor found writing to the brother easy. Janet's letter came slowly. It was easy to say thank you for the chocolates, it was harder to phrase the words 'Next time you are in London, contact friends of Vine Street Mission'.

Fate had been kind to Jonathan, his health remained robust, he knew of a dozen charities who offered practical help, food, clothing and shelter. Eighteen months after leaving home penniless, starved, ill-tempered, he remembered how his wife hated him spending hours writing novels which got nowhere. The thought drove to write.

On park benches, he fought with the wind, a library refused him admission, he was turned out of a railway waiting room. With hundreds of sheets of draft notes he found refuge in St Michael's church.

The Rev Paul Dobell saw him and gave orders to his church wardens not to interfere. Later moved by an inner spirit he approached Jonathan, asking, 'Is anyone going to type that for you?'
Jonathan jolted out of his mood, stuttered, 'I - I.'
'Is it a novel or an autobiography?' The minister slowly picked up several loose sheets of foolscap and listened as Jonathan continued.
'Sorry, I should not have sat here, I've no right here, I'm keeping others out.'

Listening to a catalogue of apologies the minister glanced at the author's work, the words came easily to his eye and heart. 'I do know someone who would love to see this,' pausing, he placed the sheets in his hand on the pew. 'No sale - no fee' was a plea and a prayer.

In the years which followed, Jonathan found mental relief in writing until, just after our story started, the publisher asked, 'Have you seen Jonathan?'
'No why?'
'We have not heard from him for six months and he promised us the last chapter.'

Mr Taylor's letter gave him Jonathan's wife's address and inspired Janet to suggest they paid her a visit. Mr Taylor seized what he saw as a golden opportunity for a day out with Janet.

When they reached Mrs Willett's address, they were not prepared to find the entrance gate locked and guarded nor the front door padlocked within. An hour with the matron and Janet came away in tears, happy to have a shoulder to lean on.

Shortly after they left, Rev Dobell rang the doorbell with the same request.
'Did Mr Willetts ask you to call?' The matron's face betrayed no secret.
'No, others told me she was an inmate.'
'She was on the staff.'
'Was?' Rev Dobell queried.
'She was very badly disfigured and never went outside these walls - everybody loved her.'
'Did she do it?'
'He blames himself, they had a furious quarrel and he walked out, she followed in the car and crashed.'
'You said was?'
'She died last month.'

Fortified with strong coffee the minister made his way home to be told, 'Your tramp was found this afternoon slumped in the pew.'

It was the publisher who filled in the missing details. Jonathan's first manuscript 'A tour in despair' had been well received. A second volume 'The open road' proved as profitable. The third volume needed the last chapter.

Receiving matron's letter, Jonathan rushed to St Michael's, in his mind two phrases rung clear, 'A gentleman for God - help is only a prayer, a phone call away'. In the church he tried to write, his mind clouding and clearing as he faced the fact. Years of wandering had served no purpose except to drain him emotionally and physically while his wife's suffering cheered others. As he struggled to breathe a prayer 'Lord help me'.

The Rev Dobell wrote the last chapter, a fanfare to shattered dreams, perhaps tomorrow another will add a postscript, 'on a higher plane'.

No Thanks For The Memory

M F Base

Wistfully looking back I suppose no one would have called me handsome or even slightly good looking, particularly when compared to some of my contemporaries which, let's face it, are certainly more pleasing to the eye, usually conceived in shiny, immaculate leather or some similar plastic material together with plated fittings and sometimes incorporating the latest in secure combination locks!

But, nevertheless, though I may have looked old fashioned, cheap and perhaps a little shabby at times, looks can deceive and what I may have lacked in elegance and good looks has been more than compensated for by the service I have freely given combined with an ability to survive the knocks and abuse to which I have been subjected to over the years!

During my busy working life, both home and abroad, I was a constant and loyal companion to my owner and uncomplaining of the treatment periodically received as I was man-handled and on occasions flung willy-nilly into whatever was to be my temporary resting place!

And in my time I have contained many and devious items, among them papers, documents and minutes from both the workplace and/or some committee or other on which I was serving at that particular time. Plus, at various times, cigarettes, cigars, sweets, chocolates and sandwiches, a variety of pills, both medical and otherwise, not forgetting pens and pencils, calculators, spare spectacles etc! In fact, all in all, an elixir of life's needs for those, like my owner, constantly on the move!

Even at holiday time when one would expect to be resting, I was usually pressed into service to find some of the usual items withdrawn to be replaced by all and everything not considered suitable for, or were surplus to, the normal holiday luggage! In this category came passports and tickets, razors and pyjamas (usually male) books and magazines, dental appendages and smellies, unique holiday pills and so on ad-infinitum!

As is usual I suppose, cleaning me out even occasionally was never attempted or for that matter even thought about it would seem! As a result and after a year or two of such neglect, conditions became a little uncomfortable to say the least with everything sloshing around in a mixture of paper clips, fluff and dust and the mess of other unmentionable and sundry items!

Regretfully, it seemed to me that my real worth was never fully appreciated until in the end I now stand here forlorn, somewhat the worse for wear and past my 'sell-by-date', reposing in this remote and draughty cupboard!

Even in this situation, tired and fed up as I am, and it would seem, largely forgotten, I am apparently still expected to 'do my bit' and provide a home for the multitude of old papers and other outdated rubbish which has accumulated over the years, plus the usual assortment of miscellaneous surplus items no longer required among which, it would seem, includes 'me'!

Before I finally disintegrate, is there anybody out there willing to shake my handle and thank me for long and faithful service?
Anybody? Anyb . . . ? An . . . '
Well what did you expect? Gratitude? Not bl . . . likely!

THE SHOW AND LIFE

John Whelan

The juggler advanced to the edge of the circus ring. The coloured balls rising and falling in mesmeric arcs, the tiny girl never taking her eyes off him.

In those long moments 'Romany Brown - The Incredible Juggling Gypsy' as he was billed on the colourful posters - seemed to hold her entire universe in his grasp. Her eyes never left his smiling face or the circling orbs which for her represented that universe.

The gypsy poised himself on the perimeter immediately before the child. He placed first one foot, then the other on its raised edge, the balls ever circling, towering over her. Several clowns and acrobats filled the rest of the ring with their own particular magic for the enjoyment of the appreciative audience. But just here in a world all of its own, a more personal drama was taking place.

The child clapped her hands together in delight at the gypsy's adept performance, her golden hair caressed by the edge of the spotlight and her angelic face intent in that delight.

The gypsy bowed to her innocence and joy and dropped a ball, a red one. She was struck intensely by this minor disaster, but as the ball bounced once she instinctively reached out and caught it, did not shrink back, and his smile in that split second still never wavered.

The gypsy stepped down into the ring and backed away towards its centre, still juggling. And still holding hypnotically, her absolute attention. Until joining the other performers, he finally gathered in the balls with an elaborate flourish.

The applause rose to a crescendo, the performers bowed in the centre of the ring and with a last personal salute to her, Romany Brown raised his hand and was gone. With him went the child's sorrow at his leave-taking.

Watching both of them, equally mesmerised, the man who sat beside her, his protective arm across the back of her seat, had sensed something was about to happen.

The gypsy had caught his eye, held it a moment before turning away. But not before a shared joy, a shared sorrow passed between them. The watching man believing himself to be the child's father, saw the loop of rapture on her face, so young, so alive, so happy, and her dancing blue eyes as she held the red ball out to him. He now wondered why he had ever considered it important whether he was her father or not. He had loved her mother and would raise the child as his own, for since her mother's passing he knew he meant everything to her.

He placed his arm around her small shoulders and drew her to him.

MAN AND BOY
David Daniels

'Tommy, come out from behind that chair!'
Tommy didn't like what he saw. That grown-up had wheels; why wheels? It was just silly.
'Out now!'
He stumbled out, falling face down on the grubby deep pile carpet.
'This is your Uncle Frank - he's my brother. He's come to stay with us.'

Tommy looked up at his mother, smiling with her teeth and then at the man with wheels. What a funny man: his legs were all thin and bendy; he had hair the colour of clouds, but it stuck out from his head; his eyes popped out too, funny eyes with lines inside them like when Tommy cut himself. He had a thick woolly jumper on, with lots of holes and he kept scratching the hairs on his face. No, Tommy didn't like how this man looked, this funny man.

'Now Mrs Harris, this really isn't good enough.'
'What is it, does he misbehave?'
'If that was all . . . hmmph,' the headmistress cleared her throat: 'he doesn't speak, not a word.' She glared at Tommy's mother, like it was her fault!
'But he doesn't, I mean -'
'Perhaps the doctor -?'
'Oh er, no. There isn't anything wrong with him; you see, he just doesn't like talking.'
'But how does he communicate? We haven't the facilities to cater for ahem . . . awkward children, you see, it upsets the other children.' The headmistress strode across to the window, framing herself in bright sunshine, silhouetting her features.
'Awkward, *awkward!* He's a five year old child; he's a little boy lacking in confidence who needs our help and support. He understands signs . . . well, sometimes; he's just shy. A little *understanding.'*
'We *are* trying. His writing and arithmetic are excellent; but no special treatment. I'm willing to be patient.'
'If it ain't broke, as they say . . . '

Tommy's mother returned to the living room, ornate tray and tea service in hand. 'How long is it now, then, Frank?'

'What?'
'You've been here.'
'Two years, maybe a little more.'
'Seems . . . '
'Longer?'
'I meant to say, didn't seem . . . seen Tommy today?'
'He's upstairs. Thought I'd take him for a wal - huh, run today.'
'Walk is fine: after all, that's what he's doing.'
'Growing up so *quickly*.'

Tommy jumped down the stairs one at a time with his grubby football cradled in the crook of his arm. He looked up as he saw his Uncle sitting by the settee.
'Coming for a walk?'
Tommy popped his eyes, then following the rolling chariot out to the hall, eyes twinkling as he watched the scruffy man stretch up and struggle with the door lock.

They walked together, Tommy half-running, down the long convex slope toward town. Tommy saw a woman changing in a fashionable clothes' shop and stood there, fascinated: the partly open curtain just enough . . .
'Hey, what are you up to? So, a ladies' man it is. Come on, let's go and get an ice-cream.' After buying two of the van variety, Frank placed Tommy's hand on the chair's armrest and launched the apparatus off the kerb and across the village square; the tinkly music got more unbearable the closer he approached: Frank put his fingers in his ears and grinned at his nephew - a craft fair had set itself up on the bank running down to the river; Tommy's eyes jerked from scene to scene, Frank smiling as wonder remained, didn't want to wane. They both moved smoothly along the line of stalls: fortune tellers, fire breathers, craft stalls, people making furniture on a hand lathe, a mock medieval battle, an archery contest with realistic 'Robin Hood-style' costumes, a marquee selling barbecued organic produce and best of all acrobats; Frank grabbed a pop, tea and burgers and chips for two.

Nephew Tommy had moved: a brief panic and Frank stopped when he saw his nephew frozen, mesmerised by the tumbling, juggling and colours. Three drunken youths passed either side of himself and

Tommy, one bumping Frank's elbow: half the contents of Frank's drink fell into his lap. None of the youths acknowledged Frank or his charge; sending forth expletives and profanities changed that: the response ended in 'Gran'pa'.

'What's a git, Uncle Frank?'

The remainder of Frank's drink ended over his knees, framed by watering eyes and coughing.

'Hrmpph,' he cleared his throat, 'well, I think a git is someone who doesn't care what he does or says, ignoring the effect on the people around him.'

'Are there always three of them, Uncle?'

'Where, where?' Frank said, winking and smirking at Tommy; the smile said all friend and his nephew drew close and grabbed his sleeve with little hands.

'Do gits say prayers, Uncle?'

Frank trembled, thanking whoever for an empty bladder: 'Do you like people who say prayers?' he managed, still holding back, started the chariot rolling over the sawdust path with Tommy in tandem, to ease the strain on his face and throat.

'I think I like everyone, only some make me a little frightened because their eyes say they're angry.'

'But you know they're not angry with you,' he said, emphasising the last.

'Well, I think, but I don't know. I do a lot of thinking but I don't know what my thin-'

'Thoughts,' his Uncle beamed at him.

'- thoughts mean. Will I be a git?'

'Oh, no, you have too many friends and family who like you. Am I a git?'

'Oh, no,' said Tommy impassively, 'you're just a dirty, smelly, old man on wheels.'

'*My friend*,' said Frank chuckling.

'Like to know your fortune?' a wizened old woman said.

Tommy liked her colourful swishing skirt that rattled and her big earrings. Frank stopped and turned toward Gypsy Rosie's tent; Tommy just stared.

'Your hands please . . . thank you. Ahh, I see good fortune - you have recently made a new friend.'

Frank beamed at the woman and then at Tommy. Tommy smiled back briefly, too fascinated to do otherwise.
'But treasure today.'
'That's a bit vague, what else?' grumbled Frank, sticking out his chin.
'That'll be two pounds, please.'
Tommy lined up for a go.
'No, lad, you're too young for this silly stuff.'
The woman glowered at him as he rotated and carried on with his nephew.

Frank took Tommy along the unoccupied remainder of the field and pointed out jackdaws, sparrows, blackbirds and thrushes; Tommy wanted to know why so many birds had fat bellies.
'They're for them to keep lots of worms in,' said Frank; his nephew's reaction was instant acceptance and understanding.

They got fish and chips after a while and Frank showed Tommy how to take out the bones without getting in a mess.
'Here, try this,' holding out a white spherical object.
'Yuck, errr, what is it?'
'A pickled onion . . . God's food.'
'Do they come from God? He can't be very clever, all his food should taste yummy and not make you pump: my friend David said that.' He put a hand over his mouth, then thought of something else: 'Does God like pumping, Uncle?'
'Best farter around,' said Frank, smirking as he pulled himself back up the bank; 'what do you want to do now?'
'Can I go on the bumper cars?'
'Sure. You're like me, they're my favourite too.'

They stood a while in the queue, not helped by some of the youths having double turns but eventually Tommy jumped into one: past its 'sell-by-date', the car's wrap-around bumpers had started to peel.

'Sorry, he's too young,' a serious-looking staff man moaned.
Frank held up his arms in resignation, then looked fiercely at the man. Tall, skinny and laid-back, the man looked first at Tommy, then at Frank:
'Okay, I'll take him around,' he said as he dropped his shoulders.

'See, you *can* be nice . . . sometimes,' mumbled Frank, tongue firmly pressed into cheek. He rotated to change position before he could see the response.

A klaxon sounded as the cars started up, Tommy gripping the sill in front, jerking back and forth to make the car go faster; the assistant steered the car around in what Frank thought were boring circles: 'Come on, give it some, knock him into next week!' Frank's response to a large man bumping into the back of his nephew's car wasn't appreciated by the assistant, who glared at him again over his shoulder: too long - he was sandwiched between two cars sideways on.

'What a wuss,' Frank said, turning down his mouth and sneering; his nephew just looked at the driver of his car like he was mad.

The assistant continued to avoid other cars apart from the occasional bump; Tommy was in danger of falling asleep. The ride ended, to Frank, properly, with the assistant stranded in the middle of the pack of cars, half of which were pointed directly at him.

'Mmmh,' Frank said: 'thank you,' said grudgingly sounded much better. The assistant frowned, lowered his head and walked away.
'He's a very bo-oring man, Uncle.'
'Let's go,' said Frank, 'call me Frank if you want,' smiling with his eyes at Tommy. 'Like to walk along the river before we go home?'
'Yes - yes, please.'

They walked a quarter mile along the river towpath, passing afternoon pub crowds, people gardening and, to Tommy's joy a group of boys playing with toy boats. Frank wheeled up the bank to a small shop, looking in the window before he went in. Two minutes later he came out with a brown package. 'Here you are; have fun.'
Tommy tore open the package, his eyes lighting up at what he saw: 'What are those two levers on top of the black box for, Uncle?'
Frank popped his eyes, hesitating: 'F-firing torpedoes!'
'Whoahh,' Tommy squealed, running full speed to the bank.
'Careful now when you put it in - don't bend over the water too far.'

Tommy switched the motor on with the control and steered the submarine straight for the largest boat: submerging, he manoeuvred it expertly into line and flicked a lever: there was silence as the boys continued their pedestrian pursuit, then a cracking noise as the big boat heeled over and settled in an undignified slant on the mud of the lake.

A small, puny boy, immaculately dressed looked at Tommy with hate, then 'Waaah, look, waaaah!'
'- told him many times about them,' said Frank, looking far away.
The unlucky boy stopped crying: 'What, mister?' rubbing his eyes.
'Rocks, bloody rocks. Told the park keeper dozens of times about them: shallow pond, sharp rocks; that might have been a boy or girl hitting them.' He half winked at his nephew as all other eyes looked accusingly at the pond, then headed for the keeper's hut.
'You think good, Frank,' Tommy said, grabbing his boat and gripping his Uncle's chariot as they tore up the hill and out of the park.

'Good day, then, Frank?' said his sister when they arrived home, 'you been running?'
'Just -' Frank gulped, 'practising breathing.' He beamed at Tommy as his sister turned away.

That night Tommy dreamt of lots of things but mostly of his adventures with Frank.

In the morning, he found his mother talking rapidly on the phone; her face was wet. Afterwards she crouched down: 'He wouldn't know anything, son, just passed away when sleeping. Uncle Frank was a nice man, smelly and dirty, but a nice man.'

Tommy sobbed a little as he ran upstairs and pulled out his notebook. He began, 'Yesterday, I went out with a nice git . . . '

A Second Chance

Bill Adams

Laura and Debbie had been best friends since their schooldays. It was an usual friendship.

Debbie from her teens had been a bit of a tearaway. Brought up in a family with four older brothers had probably influenced her lifestyle. She excelled in sporting activities and was the life and soul of parties. Academic subjects were low on her list of priorities but she somehow managed to scrape through her exams with Laura's help.

Laura, in complete contrast hated sports but excelled academically. She was always seen with her 'head in a book', a right little swot.

Unlike Debbie who was usually loosely garbed in garish colours, Laura was always so 'prim and proper', neatly attired, never a hair out of place.

After they were married, within a month of each other, they met every Friday morning for a gossip over coffee at Mrs T's cafe in the High Street.

Both had been married for only a short time so the gossip was chiefly about their husbands' 'performances'.

Debbie's marriage had followed quickly after a holiday romance on an 18-30 club holiday in Spain where she had met Steve, 'a hunk of Yorkshire' as he had described himself when first introduced. The son of a farmer, he was built like a bull, had an insatiable appetite for everything from liquids to solids and consumed Debbie from the moment she had come into his sights.

But Debbie was also a country lass, tall, blonde and buxom. An ardent supporter of the local rugby league club, she was always ready for a rough and tumble.

Before, during and after the honeymoon every day had been like a trip to an adventure park. Steven had an inexhaustible supply of energy, bursting with vitality that she could only match by consuming cocktails of vitamins and attending regular aerobic classes at the local leisure centre.

Money was no problem as Steve had his own thriving building construction business with a reputation for quality workmanship. He worked irregular hours and would often appear home at odd times of the day and whisk her away on some hair-brained adventure. So when it came to discussing husbands' 'performances' at coffee times, on a scale of one to ten, her Steve always achieved ten plus.

In contrast Laura's marriage had from the start swung from highs to lows and of late mostly lows.

She had met Ralph when he visited the clothing factory where she was employed as a personal secretary to the manager. His firm had obtained the contract to convert the outdated accounting machines to the latest computers. He was the chief technician and supervised the installation.

She had met him briefly once before at a management meeting when the decision to accept his firm's tender had been made.

Although well dressed and extremely knowledgeable about computers she thought he had a 'shifty' look about him so made some discreet enquiries into his background. She was surprised to learn that in his teens he had been an electronics whizz-kid and had designed several improvements to computers and related software. His present firm had recognised his potential and had employed him in their special projects section and soon after he was promoted to their chief technician. Quite an impressive record she thought especially for someone so young. But there was still something about him she didn't like.

So when the installation had been completed she was somewhat taken aback when as he was leaving he approached her and asked her out to dinner that evening. She was not normally at a loss for words but the surprise was so great she just stared at him in astonishment. He immediately took advantage of her silence and as he turned to walk away said, 'I'll call for you at your home at 7.30 sharp - I know the address - it's on the computer.'

Well that's how the relationship began.

That evening he turned up in his Vauxhall Vectra half an hour late and offered no apologies. Laura was in a bad mood for starters and by the time they reached the dessert she had listened to his life story and was regretting that she had accepted his invitation. The only plus was that with his incessant chatter she hadn't had to talk, just nod her head in the right direction when it seemed appropriate to do so and she had been able to enjoy the superb meal.

He must have been impressed by her non vocal contribution to the 'conversation' because he asked her if they could have a repeat performance.

Well, she thought why turn him down. The offer of another superb meal with no commitment other than to just be a good listener was acceptable, and so it progressed. That's not quite the right word though. He might have thought that he was making progress but as far as she was concerned she was beginning to get bored with all the one-sided conversation and by now had heard all about his life from the cradle to that morning's breakfast. But they continued to meet for a meal and a 'chat'.

As she told Debbie many times later at their coffee mornings she must have been comatose the day he had asked her to marry him and she had accepted.

After a motoring honeymoon touring the vineyards of France they set up home in a newly built executive style house in a select part of the town.

From the beginning Ralph had started dictating and organising her daily routine. She should have guessed it. Firstly she was no longer to work but to be at home at all times to provide for his needs. She hadn't objected at first because it seemed an acceptable novelty. But she soon became bored with the domestic routine and suggested she sought part-time employment. But he wouldn't hear of it, although he relented a little while later by suggesting she could take up some charitable work at the local hospital or church but only in the mornings. Laura didn't like the idea and said so.

The months soon passed and she had hardly made a decision herself. Then the unusual happened. Ralph started working late and became less demanding. He started sleeping in another bedroom saying he needed more rest and had tranquillisers from the doctor to help him sleep. Then he started staying away weekends saying that due to the recession it was necessary to search for orders in other parts of the country.

Laura didn't mind. She began a more relaxed lifestyle and enjoyed his absences. Time began to pass more quickly and soon they were to celebrate their first wedding anniversary. They had planned a celebratory dinner at the restaurant where they'd had their first meal together.

On the day before their anniversary, at their usual coffee morning, Debbie out of the blue asked Laura if she hadn't wondered why Ralph worked late so often, spent weekends away and when at home slept in a separate bedroom? Didn't she ever suspect him of having an affair?

Laura was taken aback by Debbie's suggestion and annoyed with herself that she had innocently never given it a thought. She quickly changed the subject and didn't refer to it again as they made their ways to their cars.

As she drove her old banger home she thought over what Debbie had said and reflected on Ralph's actions during the past months. What a fool she had been not to have suspected him of cheating her.

She parked the car in the drive and as she unlocked the front door heard the phone ringing. She rushed in and picked it up expecting to hear Ralph saying he would again be late home for his evening meal. But she was surprised and shocked to hear the voice of a female with a young sounding husky drawl say, 'I thought I'd better ring you before your husband comes home, it will lessen the shock when he tells you that he and I have been lovers of the past six months and I am expecting his child. He will be leaving you tomorrow to live with me.'
Before Laura could speak, the line went dead.

Shocked, she collapsed into a chair and recalled what Debbie had said that morning. Had she known more but didn't like to tell her? How could she have been so naive to have accepted without question his reasons. Shock turned to a loathing for her husband. She was amazed at the degree of hate that had suddenly welled up inside her. He wouldn't get away with it. She had to take revenge at being deceived. She would bring forward the celebratory dinner to that evening. It would be a meal he would never forget.

Her adrenaline was flowing as she planned her revenge. Every step was clear in her mind as she rushed upstairs to Ralph's bedroom for the bottle of tranquillisers he kept on his bedside table. She would grind them down into a fine powder. Each course of the meal would be his favourite and his portion would be generously laced with the powdered tranquillisers.

Saucepans bubbled away on the stove. The joint of beef sizzled in the oven. She kept the door of the kitchen open to the dining room and the hall to let the appetising aroma percolate through to the hall.

The table was beautifully laid with only the candles to be lit. Just as she was finishing preparing the dessert Ralph breezed in looking very pleased with himself. He took Laura in his arms, kissed her and said, 'That's the end of working late and weekends away, tomorrow will be the start of a new lifestyle.'
Wait for it, she thought, here comes the bombshell - but no, he continued by complimenting her on the beautifully arranged table and the aroma of good food. Oh well, she thought, he's saving the slaughter until he's had his meal.

Ralph went to the drinks cabinet and poured himself a large, neat whisky as was his custom each evening. He gulped it down.
'Have another,' said Laura, 'dinner won't be long.'
He poured another large one and sat near the fire sipping the whisky and watching Laura through the open kitchen door. Building up courage, she thought.

The candles were lit and the wine brought to the table. Laura was aware that Ralph's eyes were following her every move but it didn't unnerve her. She was surprised at her calmness.

Ralph took his seat at the table. Laura brought in the baked egg ramekins, followed by his favourite minestrone soup, both heavily laced with the powdered tranquillisers. She plied him with wine which he drank voraciously to quench his thirst after the salted soup. A bottle of red wine was opened to compliment the beef which he liked rare. The large portion of Yorkshire pudding contained the next helping of tranquillisers and the bread and butter pudding and custard the remainder of the twenty-four tranquillisers.

Not a word was said during the meal. Laura sensed that the mixture of the whisky, wine and tranquillisers were having an immediate effect because just as he was finishing the last mouthful and the last drop of wine, he spoke suddenly saying he felt hot and dizzy. He had a glazed look in his eyes and beads of perspiration appeared on his forehead. He undid his tie and loosened his collar.

'Have a brandy, it will clear your head and help settle your stomach,' said Laura, and he did. 'Have another,' said Laura pouring him a large one. He gulped it down. Then lurching from his chair, said he thought he had better go upstairs and lie down for a while.

Laura helped him up the stairs and to undress and put his pyjamas on just before he collapsed unconscious onto the bed.

She then rushed downstairs, put on a pair of rubber gloves, collected the empty tranquilliser bottle, the half empty bottles of whisky and brandy and the glasses. After carefully wiping them clean she wrapped Ralph's fingers around each of them and placed them on the bedside table. Ralph's breathing was already becoming laboured.

The deed done, Laura cleared the table, washed away all traces of the tranquillisers and acted as normally as she could. When she had finished washing the dishes and pans she settled herself in a comfortable chair by the fire and watched a film on television, then retired.

Without turning on the light she checked to see if Ralph was still breathing but couldn't tell and didn't want to touch him so withdrew to her room.

Laura lay awake most of the night rehearsing what she would say to the doctor and the police when they would come in the morning. She felt no serious qualms about what she had done. It served him right and the bitch who had stolen him from her. With such hateful thoughts in her mind she finally fell asleep, only to be rudely awakened by the ringing of the front door bell. The bedside clock showed it was 7.30am.

She put her dressing gown on and peered out of the window and saw the caller was the postman. She rushed downstairs and opened the door. The postman apologised for getting her out of bed but said he had a receipt for a packet which needed her signature. She duly signed it and was handed the packet which was addressed to her and a foolscap envelope marked, 'Confidential' addressed to Ralph.

When she opened the packet, two keys, and a ring fell to the floor. As she bent to pick them up she saw that there was also a letter inside the packet. Withdrawing it she recognised Ralph's handwriting.

'My darling Laura,' it read, 'I thought I would let you get up to answer the door to the postman while I'd pretend to be asleep. I bet you're wondering what the keys are for. Well, as it's our first wedding anniversary today I wanted to give you a special present to make up for all the late nights and weekends I've been working. I have saved the extra money and bought you a new Vauxhall Astra, you deserve it my darling for putting up with me during our first year together. It will be delivered at 9.30am so be ready and we'll go for a drive and . . . '

Laura couldn't read more as she had started sobbing uncontrollably.

After a little while she wiped the tears from her eyes and picked up the letter marked 'Confidential' addressed to Ralph and tore it open, she knew Ralph would never be able to read it now.

The headed notepaper showed it was from a Harley Street Consultant. The letter read:
' . . . following your recent examination and the specimens you provided for our tests, we regret to inform you that due to a 'congenital deformity' you will never be able to father a child . . . '

Laura suddenly felt faint and sick and collapsed to the floor. Through a misty haze, with her hands trembling she re-read the letter. 'Ralph could never father a child' - but who was the female that had telephoned her earlier and said she was expecting her husband's child? Oh no! It must have been a wrong number! Ralph had not been unfaithful to her after all. What had possessed her to suddenly distrust him and to act as judge and executioner?

Filled with remorse, she cried out, 'Please God, please, please let Ralph live.'

Stumbling up the stairs she threw open the bedroom door and was shocked and relieved to see Ralph sitting on the edge of the bed holding his head between his hands. 'Darling Laura,' he said, 'I'm so sorry but I was terribly sick all over the bed last night, I've disgraced myself, I . . .' Laura embraced him and silenced him by placing her fingers to his lips. 'My darling, my darling,' she said, 'I love you so much, everything is going to be all right, it's going to be a wonderful anniversary,' and looking upwards, silently thanked God for 'a second chance'.